HIDDEN WARRIOR

LAURIE LONDON

PRAISE FOR LAURIE LONDON

"Paranormal romance gets a sexy addition with London's sizzling series debut." Publishers Weekly on Bonded By Blood

Dark Assassin (as Assassin's Touch) Finalist, National Romance Fiction Award

"Fiery action and romance make Assassin's Touch (Dark Assassin) a Winner!" – Joyfully Reviewed

"Ms. London's world of Iron Portal is indeed enthralling. She again brought in an alpha hero to swoon over and a love story to sigh over."
   – Under the Covers Book Blog

OTHER BOOKS BY LAURIE LONDON

IRON PORTAL SERIES

Dark Assassin

Midnight Rogue

Hidden Warrior

Heartless Rebel

SWEETBLOOD WORLD

Bonded By Blood

Embraced By Blood

Tempted By Blood

Seduced By Blood

Hidden By Blood

Enticed By Blood

Unraveled By Blood

Enchanted By Blood

NOCTURNE FALLS UNIVERSE

How Knot to Marry a Vampire

A NOTE FROM THE AUTHOR

The following map is a fictional interpretation of Washington State after a big earthquake that occurred years ago in this story. I took a lot of creative license and used the actual map only as a starting point. You'll notice that coastlines, mountain ranges, islands and other elements are not exactly how they look today.

If you live here, like I do, and your area isn't depicted correctly, that's because it was destroyed by the earthquake...or it's underwater. Sorry.

IRON PORTAL REALMS

BALKIRK

BRITISH COLUMBIA

CLUCK
ISLAND

MOUNT PILCHUCK

GRANITE FALLS

VALLENBERG

THE INSTITUTE

GREENWAY

CRESTENFAHL

CRYSTAL PEAK
STATION

NEW SEATTLE

RED MOUNTAIN

ROSEVILLE

RECKLESS
MOTORSPORTS

SUMMER'S FOLLY

CASCADIA
(BARROWLANDS)

PACIFICA

IRON HAVEN

PORTLAND

DERRY'S FOLLY

CHAPTER ONE

*T*hey came for him at dusk, three dark silhouettes against the setting sun.

Although there were other prisoners here, Vince Crawford knew *he* was the reason for their arrival. He was always the reason.

An icy wind blew along the railroad tracks, bending and snapping the fir boughs like arms waving at him, mocking his imminent departure. Because the only place he was going was back to the Institute.

The men stopped at the overseer's truck, where Palmer stood in the back of the bed, lording over the place. Anyone who dared to interrupt him and his prisoners had better have a damn good reason. It didn't take long before he was gesturing wildly and pointing in this direction.

Vince cursed. Just once, he'd like to be wrong. Was that too much to ask? Figures they'd come for him *after* he'd put in a full day's work.

The other prisoners around him talked in hushed tones, wondering whom they'd come for and why. Logically, Vince knew they could be here for any of them. He wasn't the only Talent who had refused to join the army and been incarcerated here.

But it didn't matter what the Pacifican army did to him, he would never use his special abilities to help them. *Ever.*

Keetch leaned on his shovel and sneered at the new guy on their crew, a skinny kid with a pasty white complexion. "What'd you do this time, Chaddie boy? Sneak an extra piece of toast at breakfast? Refuse to take your meds?"

Chad's eyes widened and he swallowed nervously, his Adam's apple bobbing up and down. "I...I didn't do anything." He hadn't yet figured out that Keetch was a bullshitter and you had to just roll with it.

The kid couldn't be more than seventeen or eighteen years old, the same age Vince had been when he'd arrived at the Institute's prison ten years ago. He'd never forget that cold, dark day when everything had changed —his family destroyed, the future he'd dreamed of shattered.

"If he hadn't taken his meds," Vince said, "do you think they'd have waited this long to retrieve him?"

"True dat," Keetch said, grinning. "If he hadn't, he'd have fire-breathed all over your ass by now." He opened his mouth and exhaled loudly, pretending to expel flames. Several others laughed.

"I'm not a Fire-Talent," Chad mumbled under his breath, keeping his eyes downcast.

Sean paused in front of them, a railroad tie balanced twig-like across his broad shoulders. He was an ox of a man, and despite the crappy weather, shirtless. "It takes more than one missed dose of Impedio for a Talent's abilities to return. If Chad's dosage is commensurate with ours, I'd say it would take a full five or six days for it to be completely out of his system."

Keetch saluted him. "Thanks for the science lesson, professor."

Sean hadn't earned the moniker for nothing, although *geek* would've been more accurate. Before coming here, the guy had been a brilliant software developer.

Vince glanced over at the truck where Palmer and the guards were still talking. Maybe they'd come for some other reason. Or for someone else. He didn't want to think what was in store for him back at the Institute if they were here for him. He'd been down that road enough times to know it wouldn't be pleasant.

As he shoveled more gravel, he fantasized for the billionth time about taking out the guards and escaping. One or two of them, he could easily handle. He didn't spar with a makeshift heavy bag and do hundreds of pushups every day for nothing. But that would still leave the third guard, Palmer, and Palmer's guys—a couple of worthless bastards who smelled like sauerkraut and were, at the moment, trying to hide their flask. Despite their incompetence, even *they* could press a button on a comm device, and then the whole Pacifican army would be after him.

The chain around his ankle clanked loudly, a reminder that attempting to escape would be fruitless anyway. Because even if he did manage to break free and make it into the woods, the canines would quickly track him down. A fact he knew all too well.

He continued shoveling, trying to ignore the scraping, grinding noise of rocks on metal. No matter how many weeks they worked on this railway line, that sound grated on his every last nerve.

The Pacifican government had commissioned a new high-speed rail line connecting New Seattle to British Columbia and beyond. Although it had been many years since the big earthquake had destroyed much of the infrastructure, they were only just now getting around to replacing these damaged lines. In the aftermath, crime and looting had been a rampant problem, so martial law had been invoked. It had never been lifted— well, officially it had, but things hadn't changed much.

Because the tremors had caused something else to happen.

Something that the Pacifican army was eager to take advantage of.

New secret portals had opened up between Pacifica and Cascadia, a medieval-like world long-rumored to be filled with magic. The army claimed they needed a big show of force in order to keep the invaders out. But it was just an excuse for why they needed to keep up a large military presence.

Most of the public bought into the lies and propaganda. But not everyone.

Vince continued to work like a machine, pausing only to wipe the sweat from his eyes. Thing was, they *had* machines to do this shit, but the Institute preferred manual labor. Paid for their upkeep, they were told.

When Chad suddenly stopped raking, Vince looked up. The kid's eyes were like saucers, staring at something over Vince's shoulder. And then he heard the crunch of boots on the gravel behind him.

Damn. They *had* come for him. It sucked being right about these things.

He didn't bother to turn around. And they sure as hell didn't dispense any courtesy.

Electricity snapped in the air a split second before he felt the shock. Dropping the shovel, he twisted and groaned as the current sizzled through him, all the muscles in his body going rigid. The moment it stopped, strong hands grabbed him by the hair and wrenched his head back, knocking him off-balance.

"Hey bitches," Keetch yelled from the other side of the gravel pile. "Take it easy on him."

Sean dropped a railroad tie and it landed with a thud. "Yeah, he's not going anywhere."

"Back off," one of the guards ordered. "Both of you."

The guard behind Vince held him tightly as a second one snapped a steel cuff around his neck. The third guard unlocked the shackles at his ankles. He felt like a rabid dog being subdued by animal control.

"Let's go. No funny business this time." The tallest one gave the chain a jerk and laughed when Vince stumbled.

Son. Of. A. Bitch.

Vince fell to his knees, and in the process, his hands brushed against the length of chain. It was long. Long enough to do some serious damage. The jolt of electricity may have weakened his body, but not his will.

From his crouched position, he could easily launch himself at the guard, cling to his back like a scrappy MMA fighter with nothing to lose, and wrap this chain around his neck. But just before his hands closed around the links, he caught a glimpse of Sean shaking his head.

"Don't do it," the big man mouthed. "You'll just make it worse."

His nostrils flared with a deep, roiling anger as he considered the injustice of it all. Government-sanctioned kidnappings. Imprisonment. Torture. The wrongful death of a good man whose only crime was trying to protect his son.

Sean was right—it would be foolish to make a move now—but one day, he would have his revenge.

The guard shoved him forward. "Let's go. Can't keep the doctor waiting."

At the mention of the doctor, Vince gritted his teeth. If it hadn't been for Dr. Dobrynin, Vince's father would still be alive.

Loose gravel crunched underfoot as he was marched past the other prisoners. Chad looked terrified, as if they might take him next. Sean and Keetch both scowled. A few of the others looked relieved that they weren't the ones being hauled back to the Institute. Palmer stood nearby, holding the leash of his guard dog and grinning like a damn jack-o'-lantern with that gap-toothed smile of his.

The transport van hovered on the narrow two-lane road that cut through the heavily forested area. The guards shoved him into the back and clipped the chain to the ceiling. He tried to sit on the bench seat, but the collar tightened around his neck and he gasped for breath.

"Hey fellas, if you don't want me to hang myself on the way back, you might want to loosen my leash."

The tall guard, the one whose neck and head looked like a giant thumb, pointed to the mesh wire that covered the windows. "Hold onto that." Then he slammed the door.

And wouldn't you know it? They took every corner hard. He should've gone with his gut and choked that sonofabitch when he'd had the chance.

———

STALE AIR FILLED the windowless interrogation room. A stainless steel hospital gurney, positioned strategically in the corner, was a chilling reminder of what would happen if Vince didn't cooperate.

As he sat in one of the chairs, he sucked at the skin of his knuckles, torn and bruised from hanging onto the mesh wire in the transport van. Each passing minute felt like an hour. He was tired from working all day, not to mention hungry. And he had to piss like a goddamn racehorse.

He was on the verge of taking a leak in the corner when the door finally swung open. The old doctor walked in, slightly stooped and smoothing down a stray piece of his thin comb over.

Yeah. Like that was fooling anyone.

Vince clenched his fists under the table. If given the chance, he'd kill the vile bastard with his bare hands. He hated the doctor more than anyone else on the planet.

And the man knew it.

"Hello, Vincent." A loud screech filled the air as Dr.

Dobrynin pulled out the other metal chair. But instead of sitting, he tossed a large black portfolio on the table and leaned toward Vince in an obvious attempt to emphasize his position of power.

The drawings? *Again?* Vince was getting tired of this absurd routine and continued to pick at his knuckles. He'd already told the doctor everything he was *going* to tell.

"Let's have a little chat, shall we?"

As if on cue, the three guards from earlier entered the room. The thumb-headed one was pushing a cart filled with various medical implements and syringes. With a nod from the doctor, the other two guards came at Vince, grabbing at his arms and legs.

"What the hell! You're not even giving me a chance to talk first?"

"You and me?" Dr. Dobrynin stirred his finger in a tight circle. "We're done playing games, Vincent."

Oh, how he loathed the old man's use of the word *we* —as if they were a collective, working toward the same goal. The only thing he shared with the doctor was a mutual hatred of each other.

Vince managed to elbow one of the guards in the jaw, sending him sailing across the room. He kicked another one in the balls. But in the end, the three men overpowered him, and he was soon strapped to the gurney with an IV needle shoved into his vein.

Amber liquid filled the transparent tube and flooded

into his system. Almost instantly, his head began to spin and his whole body went numb.

"Oh dear, Vincent," the doctor tsked, his bushy eyebrows lifting with mock concern. "I see you've wet yourself."

"That's…what…happens when you…have to piss… and someone…shoots you full of drugs." A feeling of euphoria washed over him. "What…what have you given me?"

"My newest concoction. I think you're going to like it. Produces quite a high."

No shit. If he weren't tethered to the gurney, he would've stretched out his arms and twirled around the room like a damn fairy princess.

There was a rustle of papers and Dr. Dobrynin produced one of Vince's drawings. It was a landscape scene of a girl facing away—a beautiful, enchanting girl. She was looking wistfully at the mountains in the background.

Vince grinned widely, unable to help himself. "She's gorgeous, isn't she?"

Stop. No. Don't think of her.

Instead, he fixated his gaze on a collection of cobwebs in the far corner. What if a large spider crawled out and—

"Many years ago," Dr. Dobrynin said, "you found a portal in these mountains. We learned of your Talent when you bragged to one of your friends, whose father happened to be a high-ranking army official. Remember that?"

I wasn't bragging, he thought. Or had he just spoken those words aloud? He couldn't tell.

"Yeah, and if that friend were here right now, you wanna know what I'd do? I'd shove my fist down his throat and rip out his tongue."

The doctor pulled his lips tightly to his teeth as if he'd just smelled sour milk. "You people—you *Talents*— harbor such violence in your souls. Now, I'm going to ask you again, Vincent. Where is this portal you found when you were a teenager?"

He felt the sting of a slap on his cheek. The question. Oh yeah, about the portal.

The truth was on the tip of his tongue, dying to come out. *Have. To. Resist.* "I...don't...know."

Dr. Dobrynin thrust a finger at the drawing. "Where is this? Where did you draw it and when?"

"In my bedroom. In Granite Falls. When I...was seventeen."

The doctor made an exasperated sound and flicked the picture with his stubby middle finger. "The mountain. I want to know where *this* is."

Deep breath. Don't...tell...him. "It's...in Cascadia."

The doctor leaned forward eagerly. His eyes widened, and he licked the corners of his mouth as if he were watching porn. "And how did you get there?"

Must not— "I...went...through...a...portal."

The doctor's face twisted with excitement. "Yes, yes! And where is this portal?"

Vince turned his head away. He didn't want to look at the drawing any longer. He couldn't. It hurt too damn much. He'd been asked these questions countless times before and had refused to answer them. He wasn't about to do so today. But the combination of the truth serum and actual physical evidence about what he knew was making it harder to lie this time.

"Did you know your mother and sister are in danger?"

The sudden change in focus confused him. Vince turned back to the doctor. "They...they are?"

"Yes, terrible danger."

A tangle of emotions rose up inside him. Had his twin sister Olivia developed a Talent like he had? If so, then the army would want her too. The thought made him want to puke.

Was the doctor telling the truth about this or was he lying?

The truth. The truth is good.

The old man continued. "They've been kidnapped by a barbarian invader. One of my best men was killed trying to protect them. We have reason to believe they've been taken through a portal into Cascadia, and we need your help. Only you can save them, Vincent."

Suddenly, the whole room was spinning, the walls

flying by at an alarming speed. He could barely keep his eyes open.

"What do you…want me…to do?"

"Tell us where the portal is so we can rescue them."

Vince visualized the large rock on the mountainside, miles into the rugged forest near his childhood home. The energy ripple was what had drawn him there. He hadn't understood what it was at first. An invisible finger reaching out, beckoning him to come closer. But once he stepped through, he knew what he had found.

"The portal is…"

No, don't tell him.

"Yes, yes," the doctor prodded. "Go on."

From the moment he saw the beautiful girl on the other side of the portal, he'd been captivated by her. Raven black hair that fell past her shoulders in soft, luxurious waves. Luscious curves that were accentuated by her strange clothes. Expressive, silvery gray eyes that lit up when she laughed.

He'd lost track of how many times he'd stepped through the portal to see her. And every time, she'd been waiting for him. They used to sit under the stars and talk about their respective worlds, their hopes and dreams for the future. It was there, in Cascadia, that they'd fallen in love.

It didn't take long to convince her to come back to Pacifica with him. She shouldn't have to live with a cruel stepfather and a mother who had checked out years ago. His parents were awesome. They would love her.

But that day never came. Shortly after they'd made plans, the army discovered that he was a Talent. They came for him the day before he was to bring her back.

His heart ached with what might have been and what he had lost. Had she found someone special? At the very least, he hoped that she'd found happiness.

His head lolled to the side. The IV bag was empty. He was tired. So tired. He just wanted to sleep.

His beautiful Zara had once told him the story of the Pacifican army breaching a portal and coming into her village when she was a child. Many innocent townspeople had been killed that day, including her father, an Iron Guild warrior, who'd been mortally wounded trying to save his family.

Just like his own father.

A tear trickled down the side of his face. Damn drugs. They were making him weepy.

Dr. Dobrynin scowled. "The portal, Vincent. Where is it?"

The doctor had to be lying about Olivia and Vince's mother. Plus, Zara would be in terrible danger if he revealed the location of the secret portal. And so would their child.

The doctor was looking at Vince with the dead, dark eyes of a vulture.

Vince became fixated on three diagonal liver spots,

placed close together, right above the man's left ear. "Is that...Orion's Belt?"

"What are you talking about?" the doctor snapped.

The portal? Oh yeah...the portal.

"Suck it, Doc."

The next injection didn't hurt. At least not beyond the initial sting.

CHAPTER TWO

*S*everal months later...

A string quartet played in the background as crowds of people milled around the museum gallery where jewelry, obsidian carvings, and hand-crafted weaponry were on display in glass cases. Priceless rare artifacts. And every last one of them illegally obtained from raids into Cascadia.

Champagne flute in hand, Zara Kane stood near the far wall and glanced at her watch again. Although she'd been invited to the extravagant event, she didn't belong here. She was an outsider among the people of New Seattle. A barbarian, to be exact—that is, if she listened to the Pacifican authorities and news vlogs. Not that anyone here knew she was from Cascadia. She kept that little fact to herself.

She fought the urge to double-check the knife

holster strapped to her thigh even though she knew it was secure. She'd made sure of that.

Ten more minutes. Then she'd make her move.

"Ms. Kane?"

She turned to see a young man and woman approaching. Tall, thin and pimply, the man wore a tuxedo hemmed to the ankles, red argyle socks, and black and white wingtips. The woman was almost as tall with long, thin arms and sharp, angular features that reminded Zara of a blue heron ready to take flight.

"I thought that was you," the young man said.

He looked familiar, but she couldn't place him, and she didn't recall ever crossing paths with his female companion before.

"Uh, hello," she said, then took a quick sip of champagne to give herself a little more time to figure out who these people were since they clearly knew who she was.

"I can tell you don't recognize me," the man said bluntly. Before she had a chance to feel embarrassed, he continued. "I'm Manny, and this is Angela. Last semester, you helped me find some research materials in the library that I needed for my Cascadian antiquities class."

Ah, yes, the library.

"Of course," she said, smiling. As a college librarian specializing in Cascadian treasures, she met a lot of students, so it was no wonder she didn't immediately recognize this particular man. "I hope it was helpful."

Manny grinned. "Got an A."

"Isn't this a magnificent exhibit?" Angela asked, her eyes glittering with excitement. "The craftsmanship on the cormorant pendant in the case over there is like nothing I've ever seen before."

"It's quite an extensive collection." If you were into stolen property, that is. Which was why she was here in the first place.

"That dress is divine," Manny said, looking her up and down. Zara couldn't tell if that was an honest compliment or not. She didn't exactly have a thin, model-esque figure. "It's very Marilyn Monroe. Where did you get it?"

Zara didn't let on that she had no idea who that was. Having been raised in Cascadia, many pop culture references went completely over her head.

She glanced down at the gown's pale gray fabric. She'd picked it out because she thought the color matched her eyes. And the price was right. "At a vintage clothing store downtown."

"No! Are you *serious?*" Now it was Angela's turn to gawk. She circled Zara, making her feel like one of the artifacts on display. "I never find anything at those places. You must have an eye for spotting treasures."

She smiled. "Maybe so."

But the only treasure she cared about right now was

in the storeroom upstairs. She glanced at her watch again. The guards would be changing shifts at any minute. She needed to ditch these two and—

The other woman grabbed her shoulder like they were suddenly best friends. "Is that Birdie Lyons?"

Manny gasped. "Where?"

"Over there. You can't miss her purple fascinator." Angela pointed at a crowd of people gathered near one of the glass cases. In the center, as if she were holding court, was a platinum blonde wearing an elaborate headpiece with long tendrils of feathers that flipped and wobbled as she spoke.

Manny put a hand over his heart. "Oh my God. I love her news vlog. Did you see the one she posted last week about those church bombings?"

Angela nodded, not taking her eyes off of the woman. "So powerful. It really opened a lot of people's eyes to the brutality of the Cascadian barbarians. They're just so awful, you know?"

Zara ground her teeth and tried not to look as pissed off as she felt. So they thought her people were barbarians, and yet they coveted their beautiful artifacts. If only they knew the truth.

"Nice running into you," Manny said in a suddenly dismissive tone. Without a backward glance, he and Angela locked elbows like a couple of schoolgirls and disappeared into the crowd.

Zara exhaled slowly, felt her shoulders relax. She could only take so much Cascadia-bashing at one time.

Thank God for Birdie Lyons...whoever she was.

Time to get down to business. Zara guzzled the rest of her champagne and exited the ballroom before anyone else accosted her. Glancing around to make sure no one was watching, she trotted up the stairs as best she could in her stiletto heels.

The hallway at the top was deserted. Good. According to her calculations, she only had a few minutes left to get inside the locked storeroom, snatch the knife from its case and leave without being detected. Normally, an artifact this precious would be under heavy guard, but museum officials had no idea of its worth.

She turned to the left and had only taken a few steps when a gray-haired security guard came around the corner. Damn. She didn't want anyone to remember seeing her. Especially not someone on security detail.

"Can I help you?" he asked.

She put her hand on her stomach and grimaced. "Just looking for a restroom."

The man looked confused. "There are signs downstairs—"

"Please," she said, twisting her expression into what she hoped was a combination of pain and embarrassment. "I've got a stomach ache. A bad one.

Too many crab cakes, I guess. I really should've known better. I...uh...need a little privacy."

Gastrointestinal issues were second only to female problems on the list of uncomfortable discussions to have with a stranger. People rarely questioned them. Especially older gentlemen.

With a pinched look on his face, the guard pointed down the hallway. "Second door on the right."

"Thanks," she said weakly.

Once inside the ladies' room, she looked under the stall doors to make sure she was alone, then slipped off her heels. She should've worn flats—they'd have been easier to carry—but the instant she spotted these vintage shoes with the red soles, she'd had to have them. According to the shopkeeper, they were some fancy brand. She just liked how they looked.

She cracked open the door and peered into the hallway. The guard was gone.

Hurray for fake stomach aches.

Taking a deep breath, she centered herself, and almost immediately, a familiar rush of energy enveloped her. It skated along her skin like a warm breeze and all the little hairs on her arms stood on end.

She didn't have to glance into the mirror to see that her form had disappeared. As a Cloaking-Talent, she could blend into the background, making her virtually invisible to the human eye.

Her body still possessed mass—it wasn't like she

transformed into a wisp of air. She couldn't travel through objects, and someone could still bump into her. Only a slight ripple in the background revealed her presence. But only if you knew what you were looking for.

Cloaked and clutching her shoes, she tiptoed down the hall. Although she normally would've picked the lock, she didn't need to do that tonight because she'd appropriated a set of keys from another guard earlier. She tried four of them before finding the right one and slipped into the storeroom. After a quick glance around to make sure she was alone, she uncloaked herself. She needed to conserve her strength, because in a few minutes, she'd need all that she could get.

It didn't take long to find the Gideon knife. The *Taghta* sisters, a Cascadian religious order dedicated to preserving old relics and retrieving stolen treasures, had located the knife and needed Zara's help in recovering it.

Holy Fates, it was beautiful, she thought, turning the piece over in her hands. Sure, there were a few stones missing and the cold-forged blade needed polishing, but it wasn't anything the sisters couldn't handle. They were experts at restoration. The person who stole this knife and brought it through the portal had to have been iron sick for days…had maybe even died. She'd heard that the Pacifican army sacrificed their own soldiers to get items through a portal. Of course, the sorry new recruit would be ignorant and have no idea about iron sickness until he'd collapsed on the other side of the portal in great pain.

She lifted the hem of her gown and tucked the knife into the holster strapped to her thigh, making sure it was securely fastened. If it accidentally came loose, the connection with her broken, the knife would become visible. And an object appearing out of thin air would not exactly be a good thing.

Closing her eyes, she dug much deeper this time. Cloaking a dense metal object took a lot more energy. When she was ready, she snuck out of the storeroom, closing the door quietly behind her, and tiptoed back downstairs.

Once on the first floor, she kept to the edge of the crowds, taking care not to touch anyone or brush past anything that could move. In the foyer, she waited just beyond the reach of the automatic doors, next to a large potted plant. It wouldn't look good for the doors to open for no reason. Fortunately, Zara didn't have to wait long. As soon as a taxi pulled up outside, a couple exited the building, and she was right on their heels.

Cool, salty air blew in from the bay and brushed across her face. She glanced over her shoulder to make sure no one was following her. Even though she remained cloaked, she had to be vigilant and never let her guard down until she was ready.

A Cascadian in Pacifica could never be too careful—a

mantra the *Taghta* sisters had drilled into her when she'd decided to work for them on this side of the portal. Years ago, she'd planned to come over after falling in love with a beautiful Pacifican boy. After he left her, she still wanted to come, so when she got the opportunity, she took it.

Vince.

She felt a gnawing ache in her stomach every time she thought about the boy who'd broken her heart. He was everything she'd ever dreamed about…and then he wasn't.

She stepped into a nearby alley, uncloaked herself and put on her heels. Then she walked to the curb and hailed a taxi. Not bad for a librarian, she thought, smiling to herself. Now, if only she could get back home in time to tuck Darius into bed.

A FEW DAYS LATER, Zara glanced at the clock on the wall behind the checkout desk. Mariah, if she was coming for the knife, would be here soon. Zara grabbed the last few reference books from the to-be-shelved pile and placed them on her cart.

"Hey, Christy, if Darius comes looking for me, can you let him know that I'm down in the basement? I'll be back up in a few minutes."

She didn't like to bring her son to work, but her

regular sitter had cancelled and it was too late to make other arrangements. At least he was old enough to keep himself occupied for short periods of time. Thank the Fates that the university library hosted a children's story hour each night.

"I can put those away for you if you want to go home now," Christy offered. The pretty college student wore her red hair in two knots on the top of her head and had a colorful sleeve tattoo on one arm.

"Thanks, hon, but I've got it."

The elevator groaned and creaked like an old man being forced to stand after a long period of inactivity. When it got to the basement, Zara pushed the cart of books out before the doors snapped shut on her. She detested the elevators, with their unreliable cables and pulleys moving the steel cars up and down. But the fact of the matter was, she hated all small, confined spaces. If she didn't have the cart with her, she'd have taken the stairs.

Silence rang in her ears as she headed to the first row of books. There were probably a few students scattered among the various study carrels, but she didn't see anyone. An overhead light flickered and dimmed, casting bizarre shadows among the stacks. The place creeped her out. Not surprising, since the building used to be an old hospital with a morgue in the basement. One of the walls of the storeroom still had little square doors that opened the individual body compartments.

She shivered. Who could study down here?

But this was why she met Mariah here. The place was usually dead.

She moved among the stacks, quickly reshelving the books on the cart. All but one—a big hardcover tome with a compartment inside that held the Gideon Knife. She headed to an alcove near a seldom-used stairway and glanced at her watch. Right on time.

Every night for a week after a heist, Zara would come here and wait for her friend. Sometimes Mariah would show on the first day and sometimes the last. It would certainly be easier to arrange their meetings if Mariah had a cell phone, but the sisterhood didn't want to take the chance that their conversations might be monitored.

The elevator dinged. She knew it wasn't Mariah because the woman usually took the stairs too. Heavy footsteps echoed in the quiet. Yeah, definitely not her friend. The woman was as stealthy as a ghost.

Zara moved away from the alcove and pretended to be examining books on a nearby shelf. The overhead light dimmed again, plunging her into shadow. Although she usually loved old things, she cursed the decrepit building with its crappy wiring and angry elevators.

The footsteps got louder before grinding to a halt. She glanced down the row, expecting to see a student trying to find a book. She was going to ask if she could help, but the words caught in her throat like a hard ball of wax, and she choked.

A large figure stood at the end of her row, shoulders spanning the distance between the two shelves, face hidden in shadow. A military stance. And he was looking straight at her.

Panic hollowed out her gut. They must've found out about her somehow. But how? She'd covered her tracks well and taken every precaution. She needed to cloak herself and get the hell out of here, but she couldn't let this man see her Talent in action. Under no circumstances could she ever let anyone know what she could do.

The stairwell. She'd cloak herself there. Even if she didn't have time to run, when he opened the door, he wouldn't be able to see her.

She turned and bolted.

He barked out an order for her to stop.

Yeah. Like hell she would.

The metal door to the stairway loomed straight ahead. The elevator dinged again, the sound echoing through the basement.

Good. They had company, which meant a possible distraction. Just what she needed to—

"Mom?" a voice called from around the corner. "You down here?"

Darius!

The roar in her head sounded like a freight train. *No, baby, no!*

Without a second thought, she took off at a dead run in his direction. Just as she rounded the corner to the elevator banks, the military man stepped out of the stacks. Right in front of Darius.

Adrenaline surged in her veins. Fuck the artifacts. Fuck trying to keep her ability a secret. No one stood between her and her baby.

She dropped the heavy book and tunnel-visioned her son, ignoring the sound of the knife clattering to the floor. All she had to do was touch Darius to make both of them disappear. She'd never told him about her ability. He wasn't old enough to keep the secret yet. He'd be scared, but that couldn't be helped.

"Zara?"

That voice—there was a hint of something familiar.

She grabbed Darius's hand and centered herself. They'd disappear in three, two, one—

"Zara, it's me. Asher."

Asher? Her brother? She hadn't seen or talked to him in years. And never on this side of the portal. Was this a trick?

She whirled around to see the man drop to his knees, and he instantly became less formidable. Some of his dark hair was braided into thin plaits and gathered at his nape. He wore jeans, boots, and a plain black T-shirt.

Tears sprang to her eyes. It really was him. "Asher!"

Before he could reply, Darius wrapped his arms around her waist. "Mom, are you okay? What's wrong?"

"Shhh, baby," she said, stroking his hair. "It's okay." Unlike many ten-year-olds, he was still okay with her mommy displays of affection.

Asher reached out a hand. His face was pained. "I didn't mean to frighten you, Z-Boo. I wasn't sure that was you. It's…it's been so long. I'm sorry."

No one had called her that in years.

"And you've…got a son," he said, a tinge of awe in his tone. She could tell he wanted to say more but was hesitant because Darius was clearly rattled.

She kissed the top of her son's blond head. "Everything's fine, buddy, okay?"

"It is?"

Nodding, she picked up the book and the knife. "This is my brother. Your uncle Asher."

At that, Asher dropped to all fours like a horse or a dog and gave a goofy grin. Darius laughed.

"Why is he on his knees, Mom?" Darius stage-whispered. "He's kind of big to be doing that, don't you think?"

Before she could answer Darius or ask how Asher had found her, a woman came up behind him.

"Yeah, he is kind of big for this, isn't he?" she said warmly, her reddish-brown hair tumbling over her shoulders. "I'm so sorry, Zara. This is completely my fault. I, of all people, should've known better than to come barging in here like this. Ash wanted to wait for you upstairs, but your co-worker told us you were down here." The woman had the most beautiful mismatched eyes.

A million questions popped into Zara's mind, so she decided to start with the simplest. "Who...who are you?"

Asher got to his feet and gave Zara a big hug. Then he introduced her to Olivia, his fiancée.

Her brother, the I'm-never-settling-down guy, was getting married? Could this night be any more bizarre?

Olivia glanced around quickly to make sure no one else was listening. "Zara, I think you may know my twin brother."

"*Your* brother?" Doubtful. She didn't know a lot of people over here, and Olivia didn't look familiar. "What's his name?"

"Vince Crawford."

For the second time tonight, her heart nearly stopped.

CHAPTER THREE

Zara's apartment was located above a detached garage in a quiet neighborhood. Asher had brought his dog, a deerhound named Conry, who—surprise, surprise—was a big hit with Darius. Her son had been wanting a pet forever.

After setting Darius up with a movie in the other room, she tried to keep her hands from shaking as she returned to the kitchen.

Asher and Olivia were sitting at the small breakfast nook, which looked even smaller in contrast to her brother's big, broad physique. One muscular arm was looped around Olivia's shoulder and they were whispering intimately.

Zara's heart swelled. Her brother had had a hard time growing up with their cruel and abusive stepfather.

They both missed their real father, but Asher had been particularly close to him. Their stepfather was a poor substitute. It was nice to see that the Fates had finally been good to Asher.

She slid into the seat across from them.

"We've got a lot of catching up to do," Asher said.

Yes, they sure did. She wanted to jump right in and ask about Vince, but she forced herself not to. "How did you think to look for me over here and not back home?"

"I've been looking for you for months. Both here and over there." He pointed a thumb at his fiancée. "She was the one who found you."

"I am still so sorry for freaking you out like we did," Olivia said, shaking her head guiltily. "I lived for years with the fear that someone would discover me, so it was stupid of me not to realize that you might have the same concern." She went on to explain that she was a Healer-Talent and that she'd spent years trying to stay under the army's radar.

Zara assured her that everything was fine. She liked the vivacious young woman and didn't want her to feel guilty. "That basement always makes me a little jumpy anyway, so no worries. The building used to be a hospital, and the morgue was down there."

Olivia looked relieved. "Okay, that makes sense then. Mariah called it the morgue, too."

"You know Mariah?" Zara asked, confused. Olivia

was from Pacifica, and Mariah was from Cascadia and a member of the *Taghta* sisterhood.

"I met her in Cascadia when she...um...helped me out with something." Olivia's smirk was subtle yet unmistakable. There had to be a story behind that.

Asher grinned. "Mariah showed her how to kick my ass. So, yeah, I hate that woman."

Zara took a sip of her tea and steeled herself for her next question. As much as she enjoyed catching up on everything, their reunion could wait. "So you're Vince's sister. Is that...uh...why you're here?"

Olivia took a deep breath, glanced at Asher. "Where do I begin? Well, you know he liked to draw, right?"

Zara nodded. She'd spent hours with him while he sketched. He was a very talented artist.

"I had some of his framed artwork in my apartment," Olivia continued. "Drawings of a girl and a mountain."

"The instant I saw them," her brother said, "I recognized you."

Vince had mentioned that he drew pictures of her when he went home, but Zara hadn't known that he'd framed them. "So you had pictures of me, some random girl, in your apartment? How bizarre." She laughed, trying to make light of it even though her stomach was twisting into knots. How could she tell Olivia what Vince had done to her? Was there a tactful way to tell his sister—his twin sister—that her brother was a total asshole?

Olivia continued. "When we got word that Vince was still alive and I mentioned your name to Mariah—"

"Wait," Zara interrupted. "What do you mean *still alive*? Why would you think he was dead?"

Olivia looked confused, like Zara should've known this. "After the army came and took him away, we never saw him again. At first he sent a few letters, some poetry, but they were monitored, with blocks of text blacked out. Then one day, they stopped coming. After a while, my mother and I assumed the worst and came to the horrible conclusion that he must be dead. If he had been deployed somewhere, he'd have found a way to write or call."

Zara's heart skipped a beat, then started pounding like crazy until she could hardly hear anything else. "How…how long ago did this happen?"

"Almost ten years ago now."

She felt sick, dizzy, like she was hurling through the air, trying to find something to hold on to. Anything.

"Z-boo, what's wrong?" Asher asked, looking over at her with concern. "Are you okay?"

"Ten years ago?"

Olivia nodded.

She clasped her hands together to still the incessant shaking. It was as if someone had just told her that the world was flat. She'd built her life over here based on the belief that she'd been abandoned by the one person she'd trusted the most. She'd come to believe that the only safety nets in these two worlds were the ones you made yourself.

But now…?

"Ten years ago…" She looked at her brother and her voice caught. "Well, things were really bad at home after you left. Mom pretty much checked out from life, and Henry's drinking got worse. So I spent as little time there as possible." Tears pricked her eyes and she hitched in a breath. "That's when I met Vince. I was tending to the animals when he stepped out of the forest, confused and disoriented. If it weren't for the fact that he was naked, I would've assumed he was a local boy who'd been smoking too much prath." She attempted a light-hearted laugh, but it came out sounding flat, stilted.

Asher reached across the table and took her hand. "He came from the mountains behind the field? That's where the portal is?"

She nodded.

Asher cursed under his breath. "A portal. Literally under our noses. Can you imagine what Henry would have done had he known?"

Even though all known portals were tightly controlled by the Iron Guild, Zara had no doubt their stepfather would've figured out a way to exploit it.

"Vince and I—" She swallowed convulsively. "He

came through the portal a lot and we fell in love. He was my best friend. My soul mate. We decided to run away together, but on the day he was going to bring me over here, he never showed up. I camped out near that old *ogappa* tree forever, thinking that maybe I had mixed up the days or the time—easy to do when you're crossing between the two worlds. But he never came for me. So I figured he'd changed his mind."

She seriously felt like she could throw up.

"Oh my God, Zara," Olivia said. She lowered her voice. "He's Darius's father, isn't he?"

Zara nodded, not trusting herself to speak.

Olivia let out a long, slow breath. "So all this time, you thought my brother had deserted you, when in reality, he never came for you because the army took him away."

Zara's world was spinning. She felt as if she were hurling headfirst through a mental portal where everything in front of her was vastly different from what was behind her.

Olivia came around the table. The woman had a warm, soothing touch, not surprising for a Healer-Talent. "He would've come for you, Zara."

Part of her wanted desperately to believe it, but the past ten years hadn't been easy. Anger and resentment weren't easy bedfellows to kick to the curb at a moment's notice.

Olivia continued to rub Zara's back. "For weeks, he'd

been talking about someone he wanted me and my parents to meet. I assumed he meant one of his fishing buddies. He'd been doing a lot of fishing. Or so he said. Now that I think about it, I remember how he cleaned his room the day before the army showed up. He even made sure the toilet in our shared bathroom was clean, which—trust me—was something he never did." An affectionate smile curved her lips. "At the time, it struck me as odd, but I didn't think to question him. He was just my stupid brother. Then the army came and—well, our lives changed forever after that."

Zara shuddered. All this time, she'd thought Vince had changed his mind about her. Didn't want to be a father at such a young age. Left her, a teenage girl without a loving home or any support system, to raise their baby on her own. After all, he'd never come back through the portal after finding out he was going to be a father.

"The army took him," she repeated, trying out the words for the first time. "Took him away from Darius and me."

Vince, the boy she'd fallen hopelessly in love with, who was the father of her son, had been wrongly imprisoned for ten years.

Ten years!

The pain inside her began to morph into something different. Growing and swelling until it felt like a giant balloon in the center of her chest that was ready to burst.

She glanced around the tiny, familiar kitchen. Cheery yellow walls she'd painted herself. Gingerbread trim on the cabinets. Colorful tea towels hanging over the oven handle. In a matter of minutes, her whole world had changed and yet everything looked the same.

"Do you have any idea where he is?" she asked, her voice trembling.

"We think he's being held at a high-security facility outside of New Seattle called the Institute," Asher answered. "It's where they take all the Talents who refuse to work for the army."

She scowled at her brother. "You *think* he's there?"

"Yeah."

"But you haven't confirmed it?"

Asher explained that Rickert, his Iron Guild commander, was betrothed to a former army agent who said the Institute was where they took Talents who refused to join the army. "Neyla is waiting for confirmation from one of her former co-workers."

Zara folded her arms and stared at him. "And then what?"

"And then we'll try to drum up support within the Iron Guild to organize a raid." He talked about what weapons they would need and surmised how many men it would take, but Zara quickly tuned him out.

Wait? Try? Organize?

The words left a sour taste in her mouth. Vince had waited long enough.

VINCE STUFFED the last bite of stale bread into his mouth and rose from where he'd been sitting cross-legged on the railroad tracks.

Palmer leered at him from his perch in the back of the truck bed, a fitting throne for such an ass. "Where are you going, Crawford?"

"To water the flowers." Vince gathered up the length of chain and stepped over Sean's legs.

"I'll be watching you," the overseer growled. He curled his upper lip and spat out a long brown stream of tobacco juice between the gap in his teeth.

"Enjoy the view then."

Chain in tow, he ambled down the tracks toward a large cedar tree at the edge of the woods. The doctor had been pumping him full of drugs, so he'd been drinking a lot of water to flush them from his system. The doc hadn't been kidding when he'd said that crap gave you a new kind of high.

When he was finished and starting to walk back, something on the tracks caught his eye. Several small flowers were lying on top of the steel rails that hadn't been there a minute ago.

Okay, who was messing with him? Keetch?

He glanced down, but the poor bastard was sitting on the stack of railroad ties, right where Vince had left him.

How strange. He must've walked right past the flowers without noticing them. Had some kids been playing here earlier and left them there? Although they were out in the middle of nowhere, he supposed it was technically possible. A gust of wind stirred the flowers, and a few petals blew away. No, he decided. They hadn't been there for long.

He bent and picked them up. Small white daisies with orange centers, the kind that grew like weeds on the side of the road, their stems braided together.

A lump caught in his throat. Zara used to make daisy chains for him. Bracelets, rings, crowns. He'd spent hours sketching her as she braided the wildflowers she'd gathered. Cocking his head, he could almost hear her calling his name with the wind.

He shook his head to clear the memory. Because of the drawings, the doctor had asked all sorts of questions about Zara, so it made sense that he was hallucinating about her now. "Stupid fucking drugs."

"Vince," the wind whispered again. "It's me. Zara."

All the air left his lungs in one big rush, and he nearly fell to his knees.

Impossible.

He needed to get ahold of himself. It had to be a trick by the doctor to make him think he was talking to his long lost love. Get him to spill all his secrets, tell where the portal was located. Well, he wasn't going to fall for it. He spun on his heel to leave.

"Vince, wait. It's really me. I can cloak myself, remember?" Something cool touched his cheek, sending a jolt of awareness through his body.

He grabbed at the air and his fingers actually brushed against what felt like soft flesh. He tried to make out some sort of ripple in the air around him, but there was nothing.

She laughed softly. "Figures. I haven't seen you in ten years and the first thing you do is grab my boob."

"Zara?" he rasped, her name coming out in a scratchy whisper.

"Yes, it's me."

His heart hammered in his chest as he scanned the empty space in front of him. "What the fuck? How did you—?" He wanted to pull her into his arms and push her away at the same time. If the doctor found out that the girl from the drawings was here, the girl he'd been protecting... A cold sweat broke out on his forehead. "Do you have any clue what they'll do to you if you're caught?"

"They'd have to see me first, and that's not going to happen."

Before he could say anything else, the sound of vicious barking filled the air. The dog was still tied to Palmer's truck, but he was looking in this direction, the hair on its back raised like a mohawk. The wind had shifted direction. The dog had picked up Zara's scent.

Vince tensed and looked around in front of him, but he still couldn't see anything. Zara was completely invisible. "You need to get the hell out of here."

"Crawford," Palmer yelled from the truck, jerking at the dog's leash. The animal stopped barking. "What the hell are you doing?"

Vince cursed under his breath. "What's it look like I'm doing?" he retorted. "Knitting a blanket?"

Zara chuckled softly.

"Then stop dicking around. We've got work to do." The dog started barking again and Palmer kicked it.

"Tell him you're sick," she whispered.

"Zara, you really need to—"

"Just tell him."

"I'm sick," he called.

"What?" Palmer replied, his hand cupped to his ear.

"The doctor pumped me full of drugs. I'm…I'm sick." To sell the lie, he hunched over and held his stomach. Vince lowered his voice. "Zara, please. You must leave."

"But—"

"Get the hell out of here. Your safety means more to me than anything."

He heard a sniffle.

"I'm not leaving you," she said.

"Why?"

"Because I'm going to help you escape."

She couldn't be serious. "We won't get more than a few yards before they come after us. Believe me, I've tried."

"Then I'll cloak you. I've honed my Talents considerably since the last time you saw me."

She sounded so sure of herself and that concerned the hell out of him. "You have no idea what you're up against, Zara." He thought about the exam room with its sterile walls and medical instruments. The drugs that would block her ability. The blood. The torture. "These people are—"

"We're planning a diversion."

"*We?*"

"My brother is an Iron Guild warrior. And your sister is helping too."

He blinked, not sure he'd heard her correctly. "Olivia? She's involved in this?"

"Yes, but I'll explain everything later. What time do you usually leave to go back to the Institute?"

"Not until sundown," he heard himself say.

"And you're here every day?"

"Yes."

"Okay, good. When you see another daisy chain on the tracks, that means we're ready to go, so keep watching for it. Might be tomorrow. Might be the day after. But either way, I'll be waiting in the woods for you."

"Zara, no," he hissed. "I won't put you at risk."

"Trust me, Vince. I know what I'm doing."

Palmer yelled at him again. "Crawford!"

"Please," she said. "You have to go, but I'll be back for you."

The air around him shifted, and a few petals from the daisy chain he held fluttered to the ground.

She was gone.

CHAPTER FOUR

Zara stood in the shadows at the edge of the forest, trying not to fidget, but the bolt cutters she held were heavy. To keep them from slipping from her sweaty palms, she kept switching hands and wiping them on her jeans.

These past few days had been pure agony for her. She'd called in sick to work as there was no way she'd be able to concentrate while Asher was making the necessary arrangements. He'd tried to get her to wait until he could assemble a bigger team, but she'd refused. Said she'd do it alone if she had to. In the end, it was just him and another Iron Guild warrior, a guy named Toryn who apparently was good with explosives. Olivia had stayed back at her place with Darius.

Vince was in a group of prisoners off to her right

about a hundred feet away, and the man he'd called Palmer was pacing and barking out orders to them. He held a rifle in one hand and a leash in the other.

Holy Fates. The dog was the size of a small horse.

She wasn't cloaked. Not yet. She needed to conserve her strength in order to hide both of them if the need arose.

Asher and Toryn were on the other side of the tracks somewhere, maybe a quarter of a mile away. The plan was for them to create a diversion, giving her and Vince time to escape.

She peered around the tree again. Vince was still wielding a shovel and scooping gravel. Had he truly not seen the flowers? They'd been sitting on the tracks for almost half an hour.

Damn it, Vince. Look up.

Maybe she'd placed them too far down.

She glanced to her left and noticed that the sunset had turned the sky into beautiful shades of blue, pink and purple. Was there a glare that prevented him from seeing the flowers? Crap. She hadn't considered that. He'd told her they usually left at sundown, which meant there wasn't much time.

He hadn't changed his mind, had he?

A moment of panic seized her as she thought back to another time and place when he hadn't come and she'd been left waiting with a broken heart.

She shoved those thoughts from her head. Contrary to what she'd assumed, Vince had had no choice back then. Not like he did now. He would come.

He appeared to be arguing with Palmer now. Then, after several long, tense moments, he angrily tossed down his shovel and strode slowly in her direction, slightly hunched over.

Finally!

He put a hand on the back of one of the other prisoners as he passed by, like he was weak and needed the support. A ruse, she was certain of it. With the chain that was attached to his ankle looped in one hand, he acted as if it weighed several hundred pounds. Palmer clearly wasn't happy given his wild gestures, but Vince ignored him and continued his slow approach. Soon enough, the other man turned away and began yelling at someone else.

Even now, she could hardly believe that she'd found Vince.

After learning about the Institute, she'd cloaked herself at the guard gate and watched vehicle after vehicle come and go, unable to decide whether to follow one in or out. When a prison van loaded with men left the premises, she'd taken a chance and jumped on the bumper as it drove out to the main road. From there, she got into her car and followed a safe distance behind. After trekking several miles into the forest to where they were working, she'd nearly lost it when she spotted Vince. He'd gotten taller and had filled out so much that she almost hadn't recognized him.

After ten years of imagining Vince as the boy he had been, it was hard to reconcile her memory of a charming, sweet-natured boy with that of a hotter-than-hell, heavily muscled, tattooed man. And then to speak with him... It had taken every ounce of effort she had to keep herself cloaked and not throw herself into his arms.

Vince finally reached the flowers, and she gave a low whistle. When their eyes met, her heart stuttered in her chest. He was bearded now with chin-length, reddish-brown hair, the same shade as his twin sister's. Although there was a hardness about him that hadn't been there when they were teens, his eyes were still the same. Framed by dark brows and fringed with thick lashes, they were intense, unwavering, brave.

He gave her a nod. He was ready.

Her hands shook as she pulled the comm device from her pocket and tapped the transmit button three times. Almost immediately, she received a reply of three taps in return. Asher had gotten the message. This was it. She motioned for Vince to approach.

With a hand on his stomach, he shuffled off the tracks as if he were in great pain and needed to relieve himself. The diarrhea ruse never failed, she thought wryly.

Almost immediately, a loud explosion behind the prisoners nearly jolted her out of her skin. Vince dove into the trees as if he'd been blown off his feet. If Palmer or any of the men happened to catch a glimpse of him, they'd assume he'd merely been reacting to the explosion.

Gripping the bolt cutters, she ran to him. He withdrew something from his pocket and flicked it into the bushes. They had to work quickly. No time for small talk. Without a word, she caught a link of chain between the blades and squeezed the handles.

"Damn," she said through clenched teeth.

Vince's hands were rough and warm over hers. He exerted more pressure, and the links snapped like they were twigs. Before she could shift the bolt cutter to the steel cuff around his ankle, he lifted her to her feet. He smelled of dirt, sweat and raw man, and a thrill of adrenaline raced through her veins.

He stared at her with dark, inquiring eyes, as if he couldn't believe what he was seeing. "Who *are* you?"

Unease flared in her gut.

Sure, she'd changed since the last time he'd seen her —cut her hair, gained a few pounds. Did he really not recognize her? Was he…disappointed?

Before she knew what was happening, he grabbed her face between his callused hands and his mouth crashed over hers, stealing her breath away. His body was hard against hers. He tasted salty and wild, his beard scratchy against her face. She wanted to wrap her arms around his neck and melt into him. But then he released her so quickly that, at first, she wondered if she'd imagined the whole thing. Except that her lips felt slightly bruised.

"Come on," he growled, jerking her into the underbrush.

ZARA WAS MORE beautiful than he remembered, Vince thought as they dashed through the forest, their progress hindered by the heavy undergrowth. She wore her hair in one thick, dark braid that flicked him in the arm whenever she glanced behind them. He was surprised by the determination and focus reflected in those hauntingly gorgeous gray eyes of hers. In his memories, she'd always been so carefree and free-spirited.

Her braid hit his arm again, and he gripped her hand tighter. Behind them, the barking was getting progressively louder.

Glancing back, Vince saw that a few bushes they'd passed a moment ago were moving. Shit. The dog was on their scent and closing in. Probably had a visual.

"You're going to need to cloak both of us." He pointed to a fir tree straight ahead. One of its lower limbs looked strong enough to support both of them. "There."

He hoisted her up, pushing her lush bottom to help her as she climbed above him. They'd just reached the limb and sat down when the dog arrived, barking and leaping at the tree trunk. Zara gasped and flinched. Vince wrapped his arms around her and pulled her close.

With his nose pressed to her hair, he closed his eyes for a moment and breathed her in. She smelled like fresh rain and honeysuckle, instantly stirring up old memories of the nights they'd spent making love and staring up at the stars.

Her small hands gripped his forearms as the dog barked below them, foam and saliva flicking off its muzzle. No doubt, it would rip them to shreds if they fell. He scanned the forest but didn't see Palmer. Yet.

"How long does the cloaking process take?" he asked her.

"As soon as I focus my energy, it's instantaneous," Zara said, not taking her eyes off the dog. "You didn't happen to bring the bolt cutters, did you?"

"No, why?"

She glanced at his ankle. "To cut off the metal cuff."

He'd honestly become so accustomed to having it around his ankle while on the chain gang that he'd forgotten it was even there. "We can worry about that later."

Zara nodded, frowning slightly to herself, but before he could ask her what was wrong, they heard shouts through the trees. Palmer was coming.

She grabbed his hand and threaded her fingers through his. Almost immediately, a tingling energy traced up his arm and encompassed his entire body. The margins of his vision became slightly skewed, as if he were wearing a new set of glasses and needed to get used to them.

"There," she whispered. "We're cloaked."

"That's it?" he asked incredulously. She wasn't invisible to him like she had been before. She looked exactly the same.

Back when they were together, she'd only been able to cloak herself. He wasn't sure what he had expected, but he'd assumed it'd be...different. Like peering through a heavy veil or a cloud or something.

"Just don't let go," she said, "and he'll never see us."

"I won't let go of you, Zara." Ever.

Soon, Palmer was crashing through the underbrush. He stopped at the base of the tree and looked up to see what the dog was barking at. His brows were drawn together into one continuous line, his face red from exertion.

Zara gripped Vince tighter, her short nails digging into the back of his hand. Her skin was softer than he remembered. He stroked his thumb over hers and held his breath, hardly daring to breathe.

"Adolf, find." The man pointed into the woods.

The dog didn't budge, just kept looking up the tree and barking. Could the animal see them, Vince wondered, or was it just their scent he was responding to?

"What the hell is wrong with you? You've been doing this all week." Palmer kicked at him, but Adolf skirted out of the way. He repeated his command but the dog still refused to obey, its menacing bark leaving no doubt what it wanted to do to them.

The man made a loud sound of exasperation and moved past the tree without snapping the leash to the dog's spiked collar.

What the hell? Surely Palmer wasn't just going to leave the dog here, was he? It wouldn't hesitate to rip them to shreds if they attempted to climb down.

Zara's comm device suddenly crackled.

Vince's body went rigid, his breath catching like a tumbleweed in his dry throat. Without letting go of him, she quickly flicked off the device. She squeezed his hand twice as if to say, "I'm sorry."

Palmer spun around. With narrowed, rat-like eyes, he approached the tree again. His gaze traveled up the trunk right to where they were sitting. If Zara's cloaking didn't hold, they'd be in plain sight. Not only would they haul his ass back to the Institute, but more importantly, they'd have Zara now, too. He could hardly bear the thought of her being in the same room with the doctor.

What the holy hell was he thinking agreeing to this half-baked plan of hers?

A large blue jay cawed and flew to a nearby branch. Zara flinched, but Vince held tight. The bird cocked its head and looked straight at them, then squawked once more and flew off.

Palmer sighed and dropped his gaze. Leaning against the tree trunk, he pulled out his comm device. "Talk to me. Tell me you found him."

"Nothing," said a voice from the speaker. It sounded like Godfrey, one of Palmer's men. "It's as if he disappeared into thin air."

"Damn," Palmer muttered, shaking his head. The dog continued to bark. "Will you shut the hell up?"

"You sure Crawford isn't hiding nearby?" said Godfrey through the speaker. "Sounds as if Adolf has located him."

"Trust me. Crawford isn't here. The stupid mutt is just confused. Been pulling this shit off and on all week. Must be going senile."

"We're going to need to call this in," said the other man. "The army needs to know."

Palmer mumbled something under his breath about being fired. "Let me make a sweep on the other side of the tracks first. I thought he was on this side, but maybe with all the confusion, I got it wrong."

When the call ended, Palmer clipped the leash to the dog's collar and gave it a hard jerk. Adolf yelped as the collar's spikes dug into his neck. "Let's go, you worthless mutt."

Once they were out of sight, Zara let go of Vince's hand, and almost immediately he could tell they were no longer cloaked. The tingling sensation was gone and the edges of his vision had returned to normal. The dog continued to bark, but the sound faded as Palmer dragged it further and further away.

"Damn, that was close," he said, turning to her. "Let's get the hell—"

Zara was holding her head in her hands.

Panic shot through his veins as he gently put his arms around her again. "What's wrong?"

"It's...nothing. Just a little headache, that's all."

No, it wasn't. This had been too hard for her. "I thought you said you'd cloaked another person before."

She pointed to the steel cuff around his ankle. "Yes, but not with...dense metal objects. Makes it...more difficult."

He cursed to himself. If only he'd known. He should've cut the blasted thing off when he'd had the chance. Like she had wanted to do in the first place. Now she was paying the price.

He helped her out of the tree, but once they were on the ground, her steps faltered, and she kept a hand to her head as if to contain the pounding.

This was not going to work.

"Climb on," he ordered, crouching down in front of her.

"I'm too heavy. I'll only slow you down."

"Don't be ridiculous." Without waiting for a response, he hooked his arms behind her legs, pulled her onto his back and stood. She clung to him, leaning her head close to his. Damn, this was nice.

"Which way?" he asked, forcing himself to focus on what they needed to do to get out of here.

"South...a few miles through the forest," she whispered, her breath tickling his ear. "My car...hidden."

He headed off in that direction, trying not to make too much noise in the underbrush. He thought about the dog's erratic behavior again. It occurred to him that she might have had something to do with it. "What did you do to Adolf?"

"Been messing...with him...all week. That way, when it came time to get you, the guards would simply think the dog was confused again. The dog who cried wolf."

Clever, but foolish. "What the hell is wrong with you, Zara, coming in and toying with Adolf like that? Do you have a death wish or something?"

"I just hope they don't hurt him. It wasn't his fault."

"He's bitten me a few times, so don't feel too sorry for him."

As he jogged through the forest, he thought about the risks Zara had taken to rescue him. Did this mean she wasn't—? That something had happened to—? He quickened his pace, not wanting to think about the child she'd once carried.

After climbing down a steep ravine and crossing a small stream, they came to a gravel road. He stopped. "Which way now?"

She yawned, her sweet breath flitting across his ear, and she lifted her head from his shoulder. He almost hated to make her move. He liked feeling her so close.

"We're here already? I must have dozed off. Ummm..." She hesitated as she looked around and then pointed to the right. "My car should be around the next corner."

For the millionth time, guilt gnawed at him that he was the cause of her fatigue. Best thing he could do now was get her out of here safely and back to...to wherever she called home.

Although it would've been easier to jog down the road, he stayed inside the trees just in case.

"There it is," she said finally. He looked in the direction she was pointing and saw a faded green car hidden under a pile of branches.

He gently placed her on her feet again, but she didn't look too steady, so he kept his arms around her. She leaned against his chest and stifled a yawn. He stroked his hand down the length of her braid, savoring the feel of her soft, feminine curves pressed intimately against him.

He waited, listened. Birds chirped, insects buzzed,

and somewhere in the distance, a few coyotes were howling. Not far from the car, a doe and her baby crossed the gravel road. He let out a long breath of relief. The place was quiet, undisturbed. Which meant no Adolf. No Palmer.

After pulling off the branches from her car, he put Zara in the passenger seat and snapped her seat belt. By the time he slid behind the wheel, she'd gotten out her comm device, turned it on and gave three quick taps. Almost instantly, it was met with at least a dozen clicks in response.

Her luminous gray eyes widened as if she expected someone to jump out at them.

"Was that a warning?" Looking through the windshield, he nervously scanned every direction, half expecting to see a wall of lights come on, blasting his retinas.

"Yes," she replied, "but I'm not sure what it means. Asher told me the army will be triangulating all communications in the area, so I shouldn't try to get ahold of them on a cell phone unless it's an emergency." She looked at the screen and frowned.

"What?"

"That's odd. It's a text from your sister. She's at my place, not here." She held the device up for him to read it.

I-90 closed. Road blockade or something. D's fine. Go to Rand's.

Zara exhaled slowly. "I suppose if the army is monitoring communications, that message doesn't look too suspicious. Any innocent civilian could have sent it."

One thing was certain, he thought. They needed to get as far away from here as possible. And quickly. "Keys," he said, holding out his hand.

Zara flipped his visor down and a set fell into his lap. "You remember how to drive?"

Scowling, he gripped the steering wheel and shoved the key into the ignition. "I was seventeen. Not an infant. So where is Rand's?"

Zara sat back in the seat and closed her eyes. "He's a friend of my brother's who owns a garage and an off-road racing track. Asher stays there sometimes. We were instructed to go there if we got split up and couldn't get home."

He started the car and drove slowly down the gravel road, taking care not to kick up any dust. "What kind of lame-ass plan is that? And just who is this goddamn brother of yours anyway? The guy was a freaking idiot to put you up to this."

She jerked in her seat as if she'd been slapped. "What are you talking about?"

"He sent you in by yourself and now you're supposed to just find your own way out? Does your brother have any clue what kind of people you're up against?" His jaw clenched tight as he stared at the road ahead. "These are not grade school bullies who want to take your lunch money. They're remorseless monsters who want your life."

"He did not—"

He held up his hand. "I'm not going to argue with you, Zara. But you can sure as hell bet I'm not dropping it."

CHAPTER FIVE

They pulled into the parking lot of Reckless Motor Sports a little after midnight, and Zara breathed a sigh of relief. A man was waiting for them next to a roll-up door and directed them to park inside.

When they got out, the guy introduced himself as Rand, Asher's friend. "Can't be too careful when it comes to dicking with the army," he said with a grin. He was tall, with bulging muscles like a body builder, and wore a black T-shirt with a Reckless Motor Sports logo.

"Thanks for helping us," Zara said. "My brother speaks very highly of you."

"My pleasure." He shook Vince's hand and gave him the once over. "Sounds like you've been through a hell of a lot, bro."

Vince nodded, but said nothing. He kept looking over his shoulder as if he expected the army to come rolling into the parking lot. Maybe he'd open up and relax as soon as he felt he was safe.

"Although I haven't known your sister for nearly as long as I've known Asher," Rand was saying, "she came through for me when I really needed some help. She saved me from being the worst father in the world. I'm not sure what I would've done without her."

A knot formed in Zara's throat. It was sobering to think about all the things—big and small—that Vince had missed. Birthdays, holidays, special occasions. Darius's birth.

Rand led the way to a small studio apartment located above the end of the garage. There was a bed and an upholstered chair against one wall, and a door that led to a bathroom. No kitchenette, however. She'd need to figure out what to do about food. Vince had to be starving.

"Asher stays here when he's on this side of the portal," Rand explained, "so make yourself at home. Shower's in there. I'll be back in a minute with some clean towels."

"I'll come with you," Zara offered, thinking that Vince might want a little privacy. "Do you have any decent take-out places that deliver this late?"

Rand rubbed a hand over his jaw. "A few, yeah."

She turned to Vince. "What do you feel like eating?"

"Eat?" He blinked.

"Pizza, Chinese, teriyaki? Does any of that sound good?"

He frowned as if he were working out a complex math equation in his head. "I…um…don't know."

After being in prison, it had to be quite a shock to have choices all of a sudden. "Why don't you hop into the shower? I'll order a few different things and be back with the towels."

When she returned to the apartment a few minutes later, the shower was still running. She quickly changed the sheets on the bed and fluffed up the pillows. Grabbing the folded towels, she knocked lightly on the bathroom door. "Vince? It's me. I'm back."

He didn't answer. She took a chance and quietly stepped inside so as not to disturb him. Out of the corner of her eye, she saw his silhouette through the glass doors. That shower had to feel amazing to him. Who knew what kind of conditions he'd become accustomed to? She placed the towels near the sink and found a stash of unopened toiletries in a drawer. She set all of them out on the counter, not knowing what he wanted to use when he was done.

When she turned to leave, she noticed that he still hadn't moved from his original position. "Vince? Are you okay?"

No answer.

Zara debated whether or not she should walk out and leave him alone, but she was worried something was wrong. He'd hardly said two words since they'd arrived. She decided it was better to overstep her bounds and have him tell her to back off than for him to think she didn't care. She opened the shower door a crack and peered inside.

His hands were braced on the tile wall, head sunk between his bulky arms that were covered in tattoos. Intricate, geometric designs, all black with no color. Prison ink, she guessed, as he didn't have them back when they were together. Long, wet strands of hair curtained the side of his face, hiding it from view. Tight, sinewy ropes of muscle flanked his lean torso. The man didn't have an ounce of fat on him. He was pure muscle.

He didn't look over at her, just continued to let the water sluice over him. A few droplets splashed on her. Damn. It was frigid!

Had the hot water run out already? Only when she reached for the faucet did she realize it had been dialed to *Cold.*

What in the world, Vince?

Without thinking, she quickly adjusted the temperature, stripped off her clothes and climbed in with him.

"What are you doing?" he asked, as if noticing her presence for the first time.

"Helping you." She squeezed some shampoo into her hand, reached up and worked the lather into his hair. He said nothing as she massaged his scalp. He must be enjoying it, she thought, because his eyes were closed and he was leaning ever so slightly into her.

She'd expected to see some dirt and grime, but the suds were clean. "Did you already wash your hair?"

"Several times."

"Then why—?"

"Didn't feel clean."

Oh Vince.

She put her hands on his shoulders and guided him back under the showerhead. Rivulets of shampoo ran into his beard and then over his chiseled chest and abs. When the water ran clear, she grabbed a washcloth and squirted it with body wash.

As she washed the front of him, she tried not to look at his nakedness, but she couldn't help herself. It was as if her eyeballs were iron and the impressive length hanging between his legs was a magnet.

Crap. She needed to stop this. Think like a nurse, or something. It was just a body part.

His tattoos. She'd focus on them instead.

An intricate tribal design covered his left pectoral muscle and stretched over the curve of his shoulder. Upon closer inspection, she saw that it was actually the profile of the grim reaper with a flowing black cape.

Her gaze followed a soap bubble downward, and yep,

she found herself staring at him again. His cock was semi-hard now, jutting out magnificently, pointing straight at her. The juncture between her thighs tingled in response and her nipples stiffened.

It had been a lifetime since they'd last made love. They'd found a meadow in Cascadia filled with tiny white daisies, and when they fell onto the blanket, the stems were taller than they were. She'd brought goat cheese and fresh bread she'd made and watched with delight as he devoured it. He was always famished after he came through the portal, so along with some clothes, she always brought a lot of food for him to eat.

Most people crossing back and forth through the portals got iron sick. Even Iron Guild warriors wouldn't cross more frequently than a few weeks apart. But Vince never seemed to get sick. Sometimes she'd see him several times in one week.

The first time they had sex had been awkward. Neither of them were sure where knees and elbows were supposed to go, but they soon figured it out. Because the people of Cascadia were more open about sex than the Pacificans, she had been more knowledgeable than he was—even though they'd both been virgins. He hadn't believed her when she told him couples often engaged in sexual activity in a quiet corner of a castle courtyard or open-air market. She'd planned to sneak him in so he could see for himself, but they never got the chance.

Glancing up, she was shocked to see that he was watching her through dark, hooded eyes. A thrill raced through her body like wildfire. Her hand with the washcloth stopped moving on his upper abs.

It would be an easy matter to drop to her knees right now and take him into her mouth. He wouldn't need to think. Wouldn't need to do a thing except enjoy himself. Every fiber in her being wanted to give him pleasure, to dilute the pain of the past ten years, if only for a few moments. Maybe in some small way it would help him to start feeling normal again.

"No, Zara," he growled.

He'd guessed what she'd been thinking...and he wasn't interested.

She felt a twinge of disappointment. However this was about him, not her, and she would follow his lead. When he was ready...*if* he was ready, she'd be here for him. And that was all that mattered.

She moved to the other side of him in order to wash his back and gasped. Not only was there an open wound on his upper arm, but there were dozens of raised white scars crisscrossing his back.

How had she not seen this until now?

Because she'd been staring at his cock, she thought.

"What happened?" she asked, trying not to sound too freaked out.

He glanced at his upper arm. "A fellow inmate cut out my tracking chip."

Ah. The item he'd thrown into the woods when she was cutting off his shackles.

"What did he use? A freaking butter knife? That needs stitches."

"It's fine," he said brusquely.

"And the scars on your—"

"They're nothing."

Her breath quavered as she blinked back tears. "What did those monsters do to you, Vince?" she asked quietly.

"Nothing I couldn't handle." Then he glanced at her with hard eyes. "Listen. I don't want your pity, Zara."

His harsh tone stung, but she did her best to ignore it. "I don't pity you, Vince. I'm angry as hell at what you were forced to endure, and I'm...I'm amazed at your strength." She tentatively placed a hand on his back, and when he didn't move away from her, she traced her fingers gently over the marks. The pain. It must have been horrendous. "Why did they do such terrible things to you?"

"It wasn't nearly as terrible as what would've happened had I done what they wanted."

Her fingers hesitated on a particularly thick scar between his shoulder blades. "What did they want you to do?"

He was quiet for so long that she assumed he wasn't going to answer. It must be too agonizing for him to recount any of the horror. Not wanting to pressure him, she turned off the water and handed him a towel.

He wrapped it loosely around his waist and climbed out. Leaning over the counter, he rubbed off a circle of steam from the mirror and stared at his reflection. "They say I'm a Portal-Talent, someone who can find portals. But the only one I knew about was the one that led me to you. They wanted me to divulge its location."

"And you refused."

It was a statement, but he responded explosively, as if she'd asked a question. "Of course I refused," he spat out, gripping the edge of the counter with both hands and making his triceps bulge. "There was no way in hell I'd let them near you or...or our baby."

She clutched the towel tighter around her body. "You suffered in order to protect us?"

"A small price to pay."

He'd endured years of unimaginable torture behind bars in order to keep them safe. Yet during that same period of time, she had resented him, thinking that he had abandoned her.

She dug her nails into the soft flesh of her upper arms, relishing the pain.

After she and Darius came to Pacifica, why hadn't she tried to find him? All she had to do was locate his family and she'd have learned the truth about what had happened. Maybe she could've broken him out of prison and saved him years of torment.

She covered her face in her hands. Vince suffered because of her foolish pride.

"Don't cry," he said gruffly, touching her shoulder and then backing away.

"I can't help it."

She could feel him looking at her, then without saying another word, he left the room. How would she ever be able to tell him the truth?

She wasn't sure how long she sat on the edge of the tub before she got dressed, splashed cold water on her face, and vowed never to let pride get in her way again. When she exited the bathroom, she smelled the teriyaki and saw the sacks of take-out on the dresser near the door. Rand must have brought up the food. But none of it seemed to have been opened yet.

Vince didn't have to wait. He could've started without her. He had to be famished.

She glanced around the room, expecting to see him sitting on the bed or in the chair, but instead, he was curled up on the floor in the corner with just a fleece blanket covering him.

Oh my God. What was wrong? She flew to his side and knelt next to him, putting her hand lightly on his back. "Vince? Are you okay?"

"I'm fine," he said, pulling away from her.

Her hand hung in the air above him for a moment before she withdrew it and laid it in her lap. "What are you doing on the floor then?"

"This is where I'm sleeping."

"But there's a bed." Maybe he didn't want to share it

with her. She tried to ignore the hurt growing inside. "I can sleep on the couch, if that's the problem."

"No," he said gruffly. "This…it's what I'm used to."

She didn't understand. She thought he'd have welcomed a comfortable bed. "But…you're not in prison anymore."

He didn't reply. Just lay there, breathing quietly. She sat there, staring helplessly at his broad back that looked more like a wall, not knowing what to say or do to reach him. But seeing him here like this…it just wasn't right. Although he was inches away from her, there was a chasm between them.

Oh Vince. What can I do to help you?

"You should eat something," she said softly.

"I'm not hungry."

That couldn't possibly be true. She started to protest, but he cut her off. "Leave me alone. I'm tired. I need to sleep."

On the floor like a dog? She wanted to fling her arms around him and tell him she was sorry for not believing in him, for not coming for him sooner, but given what he'd gone through, she honestly didn't know if she deserved his forgiveness.

She grabbed a blanket and pillow from the bed and curled up next to him.

"What are you doing?" he growled, pushing up on one elbow. Damp hair hung over his face, covering one eye, making him look almost feral.

"If you're not sleeping in the bed, then neither am I."

"Don't be ridiculous, Zara. You need—"

"What's ridiculous is you sleeping on this cold, hard floor. But if you won't climb into the bed, then I'm going to sleep here with you."

He swore under his breath. "I don't remember you being this stubborn."

"Likewise."

She fidgeted around, adjusting her body an inch this way, an inch that way, trying to get comfortable. When she finally had it as good as it was going to get, she put her head on the pillow and closed her eyes.

She didn't care how long it took or what she had to do, she would stick by his side no matter what.

Warmth radiated off his body, which was good, because the floor was a freaking ice cube. She listened to his breathing, measured and steady, and wished she knew what to say. Anticipation hung in the air. He was probably waiting to see if she was really going to stay and sleep on the floor with him.

You bet I am. And I'm not moving unless you do.

Finally, he cursed again and stood up with a grunt. "Come on." He held out his hand, his biceps and chest flexing as he pulled her to her feet.

She followed him to the bed, but as soon as they climbed in, he turned his back to her, making it clear that he wasn't interested in talking...or doing anything else. But at least he wasn't on the floor.

That had to be enough for now.

VINCE STOOD in front of the mirror and ran a hand over his buzz cut and freshly shaved face. He had hoped the new look would make him feel different. Change him into a better version of his former self, someone who could be worthy of Zara.

But he still felt the same.

Dirty. Ruined. Damaged.

Who was he trying to fool anyway? He couldn't cover that shit with something as simple as a goddamn haircut. He was an idiot to think otherwise.

He slipped out of the bathroom, relieved to see that Zara was still sleeping. If she were awake, he knew he would have to ask about their child. Hell, a decent man would've already asked.

His stomach knotted as he thought back to the time when she told him she was pregnant. He'd just come through the portal and wasn't even fully dressed in the clothing she'd brought for him when she started talking. She was nervous and scared as she blurted it all out, but he'd pulled her into his arms and told her how much he loved her. Promised that they'd be together forever. Become parents together. Grow old together.

What a hollow promise that turned out to be.

He dressed quickly and headed downstairs. He

needed to clear his head, go for a run. Try to make some sense of it all. At least that deadbeat brother of hers wore roughly the same size clothes he did, so Vince had something else to put on.

Despite the early hour, the garage was bustling. A classic Skynyrd song blared through the speakers, almost drowning out the sound of an air compressor. Several cars were up on blocks. A guy in a jumpsuit was consulting papers on a clipboard. Two other similarly dressed technicians—one male, one female—were looking under a hood and arguing. No one paid any attention to Vince when he passed, which he found oddly comforting. They didn't give a shit who he was or where he was going.

A blast of cold hit him in the face when he stepped outside. Nothing like humidity to give the air an extra cold punch. As he stretched his quads, he surveyed his surroundings for the first time as a free man. He could go anywhere. Be gone for as long as he felt like being gone. No one controlled him anymore. If he wanted to keep running, there was no one to come drag him back. A week ago, he never would've thought he'd be free right now, rescued by a girl he'd once loved.

A sign for the motocross park drew his attention, so he jogged across the parking lot toward the entrance, past a few junker cars and a really nice travel trailer. It made sense to stay off the road anyway. He ran in through the main gate and stayed to the right next to the trees, where the terrain wasn't as muddy. The park was an impressive array of tracks and jumps, even though it was a virtual mud pit right now with all the recent rain.

His father would've loved this place, Vince thought wistfully as he lengthened his stride. He recalled how the two of them used to go dirt bike riding in Eastern Washington during the summer and snowmobiling in the mountains in the winter. He ached as he thought about how much he missed his father.

He ran faster, his arms and legs pumping like pistons. Finally, when he didn't think he could go any further, he stopped directly across from one of the big jumps to catch his breath. His muscles were strong from all the backbreaking work he did at the Institute, but his cardio ability sucked big time.

His thoughts kept drifting to what he'd seen in the back of Zara's car on the drive to Reckless last night. Over and over until he wondered if he'd imagined or dreamed it.

It was a child's backpack. Blue with an anime character he didn't recognize sewn to the front zippered pouch.

At a stoplight while Zara slept, he'd reached back and grabbed it. The pack couldn't have weighed more than a few pounds. Stuffed inside was a lightweight blue jacket, two library books, a plastic container with colored pencils, and a royal blue binder with lettering printed across the top in black Sharpie.

Darius Vincent Kane
Room 17
Mrs. Gandy's Fourth Grade Class

He'd nearly choked, almost waking Zara, and he nearly choked now just thinking about it again.

I have a son. A son! And he's named after me.

CHAPTER SIX

*P*almer's boot steps echoed through the empty hallway like the rhythmic ticking of a clock. He hadn't expected the hospital wing of the Institute to be this quiet. Not that he thought it would be bustling and teeming with people, but he'd figured he would see a few people milling around.

He'd gotten a message that Dr. Dobrynin wanted to speak with him, and it didn't take a rocket scientist to figure out he was going to get his ass chewed. When one of the most notorious prisoners escapes on your watch, you don't exactly expect to receive a commendation. He just hoped he still had a job when it was over.

He liked the doctor. A little eccentric at times, but he'd always been reasonable. Palmer would explain what happened—that a massive explosion knocked him off his feet, and when he got his bearings straight, Crawford was gone. If that damn dog had been better trained instead of going off half-cocked all the time, he'd have found the guy.

Palmer passed a corridor that looked exactly like one he had passed a few minutes ago. Scratching his head, he wondered if he'd taken a wrong turn somewhere. He should've reached the nurses' station by now. He paused next to an empty gurney and pulled out his cell phone to call the doctor's secretary.

"Damn." No signal.

And then he noticed the time. He was late.

He picked up his pace and walked under an arched doorway inscribed with a Latin phrase. The Institute was located in an old monastery built around the turn of the last century and then retrofitted later, which explained the confusing labyrinth of hallways.

Around the next corner, he spotted what looked to be a receptionist's desk at the end of the hallway. *Finally.* When he got there, the desk was empty, so he rested his hands on the raised counter and waited for someone to show up. After a few minutes, he grew impatient. Where was everyone?

The third door on the right was slightly ajar, a thin sliver of light streaming into the hall. Could the receptionist, nurse, or whoever was supposed to be manning the desk be in there?

"Hello?" he called, stepping toward the door. "Anyone around?"

Almost immediately, the door swung open and a beefy-looking security guard with close-cropped hair stepped out. "You Palmer?"

"Yes."

"In here."

It was a standard hospital room. White walls. Gray floors. Medical equipment with blinking lights.

And a patient in the bed.

Frowning, he glanced at the guard for an explanation, but the guy's face was unreadable.

Was this right? Why was he summoned to come here?

Then he noticed Dr. Dobrynin on the other side of the bed, leaning over the patient, his arm moving left to right. It took Palmer a moment to realize what the doctor was doing. He was brushing the woman's hair.

An awkward curiosity clawed at his insides. Who was this lady and why had the doctor summoned him here? It was damned freaky, if you asked him.

The woman was middle-aged with dull brown hair and skin the color of a moth's wings. Tubes were everywhere. Her neck. The backs of her hands. Protruding from under her bed. A thin line of spittle trailed from one corner of her mouth. Her eyes were open and she stared, unblinking, at the ceiling above Palmer's head.

He glanced down at his hands, noticing for the first time that his nails were encrusted with dirt. Had he known he was going to be inside a hospital room with an actual patient, he'd have cleaned up a little more. He shoved his hands into his pockets, suddenly wanting to leave. This didn't feel right. He shouldn't be here. He took a step backward, but the guard was right behind him.

Dr. Dobrynin looked up, his watery eyes cold and hard. "You're late."

"I'm...I'm sorry. I got lost."

"Lost," the doctor repeated, shaking his head as if he didn't quite believe it. He reached into his medical bag and pulled out a small red bottle.

Palmer assumed it was a medicine vial until the doctor unscrewed the cap, grabbed the woman's hand and began painting her nails.

Okay, this was fucking weird. If the doctor touched the urine bag dangling from the side of the bed, he was out of here.

"I got a call from the army commander," the doctor said without looking up.

Palmer was actually relieved to be talking about why he had been summoned here, because seeing the doctor dote over this patient was really creeping him out.

He wasn't surprised the CO had talked to Dobrynin. Palmer had spoken to his superior yesterday about what had happened with the prisoner. "And I told him everything, sir. I cooperated fully."

"Vince Crawford never should've been allowed off the premises. None of them should have."

And the doctor was blaming him? "But...I thought..." Palmer scratched his head. He didn't understand how the prisoners could be working on a chain gang without the doctor's approval. He was the head guy around here. Didn't he call the shots?

"And you know what else he said?" Dr. Dobrynin lifted the woman's hand and blew on her nails.

"Um, no."

"They're thinking about shutting down my program."

Palmer swallowed nervously. "But what about the prisoners?" Certainly, they weren't thinking of letting them go, were they? Those men were a danger to society. Everyone knew that. That's why they were here.

"They're questioning the effectiveness of what I'm trying to accomplish."

He didn't know what the doctor's goals were, and he didn't dare ask. Some things were best left alone. "That's not good, sir."

"You're damn right, it's not good," Dobrynin snapped. "I'm so close to a breakthrough with my research. The Impedio has been proven to work well in suppressing a Talent's abilities, and the new drug I'm developing will give us even more control over them.

What good is a Talent who refuses to do what they're told?"

Palmer had no idea what the old man was talking about. Drugs? Research? But he went along with it anyway. "You're absolutely right, sir. A drug like that is…will be…really good. I'll bet Crawford wouldn't have escaped then, right?" He was glad that they were in agreement. It made him nervous to think that he might be at odds with the doctor.

A muscle in Dr. Dobrynin's jaw twitched. He carefully placed the woman's hand on the sheet, then started on the other. "Do you know who this is, Mr. Palmer?"

"No, sir, I don't." He chewed on his lip, wishing he had a cigarette. Hell, when he got back, he was going to smoke a whole pack.

"This is my daughter, Nancy."

Palmer blinked, not sure if he should be more or less comfortable. He guessed that explained the hair-brushing and nail-painting. Sort of.

"She used to be such a happy girl," the doctor explained, his voice tinged with a hint of nostalgia. "The biggest, brightest smile. Smart as a whip."

Palmer's mind wandered as the doctor continued to extoll his daughter's accomplishments. Was there another frozen dinner in the freezer or had he eaten the last one? To be on the safe side, he should probably stop by Dick's Drive-In on the way home. He'd had a helluva last few days and deserved something special. A Dick's Deluxe with fries and a shake beat out anything frozen from a box.

The guard elbowed him in the back. He jerked his head up. The doctor was still talking. Something about the daughter's friend manifesting special abilities.

"Turns out the young lady was a Mind-Talent," the old man was saying. "And she thought it would be funny to play a trick on my Nancy. So that little brat reached into my daughter's brain and stirred everything up, leaving her a vegetable."

Palmer couldn't understand why the doctor was telling him all this. He'd worked here for three years and never once had the doctor confided anything personal. He'd had no idea the man's daughter was a patient here. "That's terrible, sir."

"Because no one knew how to control that girl, my daughter was irreparably harmed. That was forty-seven years, three months and fourteen days ago, Palmer. From that day forward, I committed myself to doing whatever it took to make sure no one else suffered like Nancy did. Those with Talents are abominations. They need to be controlled and monitored." He gave a little laugh that chilled Palmer to the bone. "If I were in charge, I'd kill them all. But I'm not, so I'm doing the next best thing."

Palmer hated Talents too. Freaked him the hell out to be working so closely with them. At least the drugs suppressed their abilities and the pay was good. By the end of the month, he'd have enough money saved to buy that fucking awesome flat screen he'd been looking at. A mammoth one, the size of a large window. Just in time to watch the biggest MMA event of the year. He planned to invite his hot neighbor over, a big, beautiful woman with curves that went on forever. And during the commercial breaks, if he was lucky, maybe she'd let him feel her tits.

He cleared his throat. "So what can I do for you?"

The doctor looked up, made eye contact with the guard. "Bradford," he said with a nod, then gave a tight-lipped smile to Palmer. "A few things, actually."

"Can you help me with this?" The guard—Bradford—grabbed a roll of black plastic. It had been leaning against the wall near the bathroom, but Palmer hadn't noticed it before.

"Yeah, sure." Palmer took an edge and stepped backward, unrolling a tarp. Were they going to be painting? Guess it shouldn't surprise him that the doctor wanted to make the room nicer for his daughter, given how he doted over her. A bright yellow would be nice. Or maybe purple. Didn't all women like purple?

The doctor adjusted some of the woman's tubes, including the urine bag. Scratch what he said about yellow. He glanced around the room and didn't see any painting supplies.

Oh Jesus. They didn't want his help with the woman, did they?

Bradford pointed to the center of the tarp. "Can you step there and flatten it out?"

Palmer hesitated. His boots were dirty. Filthy, actually, now that he looked at them.

The guy must've noticed his reluctance. "It's okay. We're just going to be throwing this away when we're done."

Palmer stepped onto the plastic and started to flatten out the creases, glad to at last be doing something. Whatever it was. The plastic rustled and Bradford bumped into him, making Palmer stagger. The man gripped his elbow to steady him.

"Hey, watch where you're—" He felt a wetness on his shirt and frowned. Had the idiot just spilled coffee on him? He glanced down and saw a growing red stain. It didn't register what had happened until the man pulled a handkerchief from an inside pocket and wiped something he was holding. A knife.

Adrenaline shot through him. This was bad. Really bad. But before he could make a move, his knees weakened, and he sunk to the plastic on all fours. "You... you stabbed me," he sputtered.

His mouth had a metallic taste, like he was sucking on a bunch of copper pennies. The throbbing in his left side turned into a stinging pain. He touched the wound, and his hand came away covered in blood.

This couldn't be happening. This couldn't be real.

Above the sound of the beeping monitors, Palmer could hear the *drip drip drip* of his blood hitting the plastic.

The plastic. How could he have been so foolish to think he'd been called here to paint? What a damn idiot.

The doctor spoke up from the bedside. "Incompetence and carelessness do not belong within my organization."

"What are you…talking about?"

"You let one of my most valuable prisoners escape."

"It wasn't…because of me." His breathing was labored. God, he was tired. He just wanted to sleep. Uttering each word was like climbing a mountain. "Dog…should've…tracked him." He coughed up blood and collapsed. The plastic was cold against his cheek.

"Always the excuses, Mr. Palmer. People these days are so concerned with not taking the blame for anything. When I was a youngster, we didn't shirk our duties. We worked hard and did as we were told. And we did it well or there'd be hell to pay." He pointed the nail polish brush at him. "So, Mr. Palmer, you only have yourself to blame for the consequences of your actions."

Palmer was cold. Very cold. He exhaled, blowing out a long, slow breath. If only he could wrap himself in a blanket and sit by a fire somewhere. The stinging sensation along his left side had gone numb, and there was a low-pitched ringing in his ears.

He was floating now, looking down at himself. The growing pool of blood glistened under the lights.

No. That was just someone who looked like Warren Wayne Palmer. It couldn't be *him* on that black plastic tarp.

Because if it were, he'd be dying.

CHAPTER SEVEN

Zara put a five-pound bag of cake flour into her shopping basket and wished she'd grabbed a grocery cart instead. She'd only planned to be here for a few minutes, but this thing was getting heavy.

It had been two days since Vince's escape. Because the road checkpoints were still in place, they couldn't risk driving to her house yet, so they were still holed up in that tiny apartment at Reckless. Plenty of time to get reacquainted with each other and to talk about everything…except that Vince had been distant, moody and had hardly said two words to her.

For the second morning in a row, she'd woken up to find him gone. Rather than waiting around like she had yesterday, she remembered that the break room had a small but decent oven, so she decided to make cupcakes. Maybe that would help bring him around.

Vince had always loved anything she baked. Bread, muffins, cookies, cakes. Just like their son.

She could almost see the excited look on Darius's face if she were home. *"Mom, you're making cupcakes again? This is another best day of my life."*

She reached for a small bottle of vanilla extract from the top shelf and thought about how much she missed her little man. She'd spoken to him briefly this morning before school and promised to call when he got home. Although it was more for her sake than his, because it sounded like he was having fun with Asher and Olivia and that sweet but odd-looking dog of theirs.

She surveyed the contents of her shopping basket. Did she really need to color the frosting? No. Darius always wanted it colored, so that was the way she always made it, but having colored frosting probably didn't matter to Vince or anyone else at Reckless. They didn't need sprinkles either, but *she* liked them.

Grabbing the small box of food coloring from the bottom of her basket, she spun around to return it to the shelf, and literally ran into the woman behind her.

"Oh my God, I'm so sorry. I didn't—" Wait. She knew her. "Mariah! What are you doing here?"

"Trying not to get run over by a crazy woman on a baking mission." Her friend's smooth black hair glistened under the artificial lights. She wore tight black pants, clunky combat boots and a man's suit jacket rolled up at the sleeves.

"Did you look for me at the library?" Zara asked. "I wish there was a way to get ahold of you. I'd have told you I wasn't going to be able to meet up this month."

"That's all right. I figured it out."

"But…how did you know I was here? No one—well, hardly anyone—knows where I am. And what about all the roadblocks?"

Mariah took a can of peas from the shelf, read the label, frowned, and put it back. "I'm good at finding things."

Zara waited for more of an explanation, but in true Mariah-fashion, there was none. Even though they'd met years ago in Cascadia at the *Taghta* abbey near Zara's hometown of Vallenberg, the woman didn't talk much about herself.

"You have the Gideon knife with you, right?"

She wondered how the woman knew that, but figured she'd get another vague explanation, so she didn't bother asking. "It's in my car."

Assuming Mariah wanted to take the artifact and be on her way, she started to leave the shopping basket in the aisle and head out to the car.

"I'm not in a hurry," her friend said. "Finish your shopping first."

"Okay. I just need a few things from the dairy case and that's it."

Mariah came with her, stopping a few times to examine random items from the shelves.

"We located another artifact that we could use your help with." Mariah squeezed a dog toy hanging from a hook as they walked past. "It was recently taken from Cascadia and smuggled over here."

"Recently? So there was another raid?" Zara felt sick to her stomach. "Were…any children taken?"

Thugs from the Pacifican army came to their world to kidnap Cascadian children in the hopes that they had Talents that could be exploited as they got older. Oftentimes, whole villages would be burned, the people killed.

Mariah shook her head. "I haven't heard that there were children taken this time."

Zara felt her shoulders relax. "I'd be happy to help recover it as long as you don't need it right away. I'm not sure what my immediate plans are going to be."

"No rush." Mariah stopped talking as a woman with a toddler pushed a shopping cart past them. "Oh hey, congratulations." She fist-bumped Zara.

"I…uh…for what?"

Mariah lowered her voice. "The prison break, silly. That was pretty damn ballsy of you."

The compliment meant a lot to her, considering Mariah herself was a badass. "I am so thankful that you told my brother how to find me."

The other woman stopped to look at a jar of pickled asparagus. "So how's this man of yours doing?" she asked, pulling it from the shelf.

Zara double-checked to make sure they were still alone. "It's hard to tell. Hasn't said a lot. He goes running, spends a lot of time by himself and sleeps. Today, he got up to go for a run and still wasn't back before I left."

"The change must be quite a shock. It's bound to take him a while to get used to life outside prison walls." Mariah made sure the asparagus jar was lined up perfectly with the rest before continuing down the aisle. "He's the father of your son, right? Because it's good that he's going through this adjustment time before he meets him."

Zara almost choked. "How did you know?"

Mariah waved her hand. "You used to talk in your sleep about a boy named Vince. Figured he was the father of the baby you were carrying. The man you helped escape from prison is named Vince, so you do the math." Mariah sniffed a candle, grimaced, and put it back. "He's having a hard time, eh?"

Zara nodded. "He hasn't asked about Darius yet, though he knew I was pregnant." She tried not to sound too disappointed, but she couldn't help it. She would've thought their child would be one of the first things he asked about.

Mariah turned to face her, a roll of duct tape in her hand. "Do you still love him?"

Zara blinked at her friend's bluntness, and the items in her basket suddenly went blurry. She wanted to shout, *Yes, of course I love him! I've always loved him, except for the ten years when I hated him.*

"I...I think so," she said instead. "But maybe I'm just in love with what we once had. It was a long time ago. We were different people then."

Mariah reached out and touched her arm. Zara couldn't help but notice how her friend's eyes sparkled like precious gems in the overhead lighting of this very plain, utilitarian grocery store.

"He's a man coming home from war, Zara. He's been traumatized. Exposed to terrible things. Experienced unspeakable horrors that you will probably never know about. Be patient and loving with him, but don't push or smother. Just be there for him when he needs you. It could take a while until he's able to reintegrate himself back into his life."

Zara nodded at her friend's wise words. "Yeah, I know."

But what if she and Vince just weren't meant to be? What if they weren't two of a kind, two halves of the same whole? It was a song he'd used to sing to her in that crazy, out-of-tune voice of his. Although he was an incredibly talented artist, Vince couldn't carry a tune if his life depended on it. She'd snort with laughter every time he sang it, which made her heart ache now. She hadn't thought about that in a long time.

"What if he doesn't love me anymore, Mariah?" She almost couldn't choke out the words.

Her friend stood there a moment, staring at her, as if she were trying to figure out what to say. "Give him time, Zara. He didn't get this way overnight. He may need to figure things out for himself first."

———————

"THAT'S GOOD," Vince called, motioning for the dump truck driver to stop. He waited off to the side as a load of gravel was dumped onto Reckless's parking lot.

Rand leaned on the backhoe, having just finished showing Vince how to use it. "I really appreciate this. I can't believe my guy who was going to do this called in sick again. He's been flaking out lately, so I shouldn't be surprised."

"No problem," Vince replied. "I'm happy there's something I can do around here to help."

"I owe you," Rand said. "Big time."

No, he didn't. More like the other way around.

"Well, holler if you need anything," the other man told him before turning and heading back into the garage.

Vince climbed into the backhoe and got to work moving gravel. It felt good to get out and do something constructive that took him away from his thoughts. He was sick of thinking. Zara was probably sick of it, too, although to her credit, she hadn't said a word about it.

He'd seen her leave about an hour ago. Rand said

she'd asked if she could get to the grocery store without running into any roadblocks. As Vince worked, he kept one eye on the entrance, waiting for her to return back safely.

Spreading gravel this way wasn't bad, he thought, as he pressed the lever to lower the bucket and scoop another load. Not bad at all. Especially since he had lots of experience doing it by hand and knew exactly how much that sucked.

He took a swig from his water bottle just as Zara pulled into the parking lot. His heart thudded in his chest that she was not only safe and sound but that she'd turned the car in this direction.

Good time for a break, he decided, so he turned off the backhoe and climbed out.

She slowed the car and rolled down her window. Damn, she was gorgeous. Her hair hung in loose curls over her shoulders, and he longed to run his fingers through it. Her eyes sparkled, a half-smile on her upturned face. After all those dark, lonely years in prison where she was all he'd dreamed about, he would never grow tired of seeing her in person like this.

"Looks like Rand's got you working hard," she said.

"Heavy equipment rocks."

"Yeah, it does," she said, her gaze sliding over him appreciatively.

His cock began to harden in response. Okay, he liked that. A lot.

He noticed grocery sacks in the back seat. "Need some help?"

"Sure."

He climbed in and directed her to park out back near the motocross park, explaining that the dump truck would be delivering a few more loads and he wanted to keep the parking lot as empty as possible.

"So you got some food?" Totally obvious for sure, but he wanted to keep talking with her—something he hadn't been good at lately.

She didn't act like she thought the question was stupid. "Thought I'd do a little baking, you know?"

Memories of how she always used to have food ready for him when he came across the portal flashed in his mind. She used to laugh and say that the portal must've made the food in his stomach vanish along with his clothes because he was always starving.

He sighed. That seemed like a lifetime ago now. They were both so young and naïve back then, oblivious of the hard times that were coming.

She parked the car, and when he went to grab the sacks from the back seat, he saw the little blue backpack again. He brushed his fingertips over the straps and wondered for the thousandth time about the boy it belonged to. The ache he felt earlier came back with a vengeance. What did his son look like? What kind of child was he? Smart, funny, serious, athletic? All of the above? But ultimately, all that mattered to him was that his son was happy.

Zara was looking at him, a curious expression on her lovely face. Jerking his hand away, he quickly grabbed the sacks and shut the car door with an elbow.

"I got you something," she said as they traipsed across gravel, not saying anything about his reaction to the backpack.

"You did?"

"Yeah, but it's nothing big, so don't be expecting that I got you a pony or anything."

He laughed.

When they got to the break room, she rummaged around in the sacks and pulled out a small package wrapped in brown butcher paper and tied with a piece of twine. She handed it to him.

"What's this?" he asked, taking it from her.

"Open it." She started unloading the groceries.

Inside the package was a pad of drawing paper and several charcoal pencils. He rubbed his hand over the front cover and then fanned the pages with his thumb. "You got this for me," he said softly.

"I wasn't sure if you still like to draw. If you don't, no big deal. I just thought—"

Overcome by the incredibly thoughtful gesture, he reached for her and pulled her into his arms. "Thank you," he mumbled into her fragrant hair. "It's perfect."

Just like she was and always had been.

She was a flame, constantly flickering in his darkness, igniting his lifeless soul for the past ten years.

"I'm glad you like it," she said against his chest. "It's not fancy. It's just—"

"It's perfect," he said again. "I'm...sorry, Zara."

She lifted her chin to him and smiled. "There's nothing for you to be sorry about." Cupping his face in her hands, she pressed her lips chastely to his. "You sketch while I bake."

Her simple kiss with no expectations made him want her all the more. He watched as she washed her hands, turned on the oven and got out a mixing bowl. She moved efficiently, as if she'd done this a hundred times before.

He opened the pad, grabbed a pencil and began drawing. He suddenly felt like talking. "Did my sister tell you anything about my mother? Is my mom...doing okay?" He held his breath as he waited for the answer.

"Your mom's doing well. It's a long story—I'll let Olivia tell you the whole thing when you see her—but your mom found out she was actually born in Cascadia. Olivia and Asher brought her across the portal to meet her long lost relatives—cousins, I think—so that's where she is now."

His mom must've been so thrilled to learn this. Relieved that she was doing fine, he felt some of the built-up tension seeping from his shoulders. There was so much to get caught up on. He knew his mother had been adopted when she was a baby, but he'd had no idea she was from Cascadia.

"That means I've got Cascadian blood too," he said, keeping his voice low in case someone came into the break room.

Zara nodded. "*Fata-blood,* given that you're a Talent. The magic blood of the Fates."

Those who had it often developed special abilities of the Fates and could pass along that trait to their descendants. This was why the Pacifican army was so desperate. Since you couldn't control who had the magic blood of the Fates, the next best thing was to control those who had it and exploit them for your own purposes. Unless they refused.

He scrubbed a hand over his face, trying to get a handle on everything. He had expected things to be a bit different after ten years, but the foundation of everything he'd come to know had radically changed in his absence.

"And you?" he asked, his voice husky. "How have you been?" He was painfully aware that these were questions he should have asked her already.

"Me? I'm...I'm good." Her tone was light and upbeat, but her hands trembled slightly as she measured the cupcake ingredients into the bowl. She told him about her job at the research library and what she did for the *Taghta* sisterhood. "I use my Talent to take back precious artifacts that have been stolen from Cascadia."

He narrowed his eyes. "*Take?*"

"Okay, steal. I sneak in and steal back items that have been stolen from Cascadia. You'd be surprised to learn of all the precious items in various private collections. There's a black market over here among the rich and privileged."

No wonder she'd been so confident she could help him escape—she'd been eluding the authorities for years. However, that still didn't excuse her brother for letting her go in alone. That fact continued to irritate the hell out of him.

She continued. "The history around many of the artifacts is very fascinating. I once actually held a sword owned by one of the brothers in the Obsidian wars."

Like most people who grew up in Pacifica, his knowledge of this part of their history was limited. "That was back when the Fates stepped in to end the wars by dividing up the world, right?"

"You actually remembered," she said, beaming as she poured the batter into the muffin tins. "I wasn't sure how much of my so-called history lessons you'd been paying attention to."

"Of course I remember what I learned during our lessons. Some lessons more vividly than others, though," he said with a wicked grin.

A big glob of batter landed between the tins. He'd caught her off guard. Although he couldn't see her face, he imagined she was blushing.

"Do you bake a lot for Darius?" he blurted without thinking.

Damn. He wasn't ready to ask about his son. At least, not yet. His hands were sweaty, and the pencil slipped from his grip.

She looked up, a surprised expression on her face. Then, just as quickly, she grabbed the pan, put it in the oven and set the timer. "Yeah, I do. When he gets home from school and finds cookies or cupcakes, he always tells me it's the best day ever." She gave a little laugh. "We have a lot of *best days ever*."

Vince cleared his throat, trying to make the sudden lump disappear. "What's he like?" he asked softly. "My son." It was the first time he'd uttered those words aloud.

Her gaze met his, and her beautiful face lit up with a tender smile. "He's...he's an amazing boy, Vince. You'll love him. He's smart, happy, goofy. He loves to read and research random things online." She shook her head, evidently remembering something funny. "He knows all the player stats for New Seattle's soccer team. He loves to draw—oh my gosh, you should see this picture he drew recently of an elephant. It's pretty amazing. Oh, and he's very stubborn—just like his father."

It felt as if he'd just been slapped. He'd been listening, enraptured, until now. He didn't want his son to be like him. *He* was damaged and fucked up. He wanted their son to be like *her*.

Vince rose and came up behind her, brushing the silky raven locks from her shoulder. "You're amazing, Zara. Just like he is. But I know it wasn't easy." He pressed his lips to the back of her neck and felt her shiver. He inhaled deeply, pulling her sweet scent into his lungs. "Sorry I wasn't there. I would've done anything to have been there with you...and him."

She placed a cool hand over his. "I know you would have."

He turned her around to face him. Her gray eyes glittered with emotion as she looked up at him.

"You came for me." He was still so blown away by that and probably always would be. "Thank you."

"I would've come earlier had I known."

He had no doubt that was true. He grasped her around the waist, lifted her up and set her on the counter. She inhaled sharply when he stepped between her legs.

"God, I missed you," he said, his voice as rough as the gravel outside.

He tangled his fingers in her luxurious hair, pulled her head back and kissed her. Hard. With all the pent up emotion he'd been feeling. He'd wanted to kiss her tenderly, but he found he didn't have the willpower. Ten years had been an awfully long time, and she was so beautiful. He'd been with no one since her. Thought of no one but her.

Life had moved on for her, while he'd remained

static. Had she loved anyone else? Been with anyone else? He pushed his tongue past the seam of her lips, wanting to possess her with this kiss. Make her forget about any man she'd been with since they'd been apart.

God, she tasted good.

She gave a little moan, slid her arms around his neck and scooted her bottom closer, pressing herself against his growing erection. He considered taking her right here in the break room. How long until someone walked in on them? Was there enough time? Probably not, but then he sure as hell didn't need much. However, the apartment upstairs would be better.

But just as he thought about grabbing her hand and leading her there, he heard the door to the garage open and several people talking. One was Rand, but he didn't recognize the other two—a man and a woman.

Zara smiled and held a finger to her lips. "Shhh."

"I already told you," Rand said loudly. He sounded exasperated. "No one has brought in a car like that recently."

"Are you sure?" the woman asked.

"Positive."

"We'd like to examine your records anyway," the man said.

"You honestly think one of my customers had something to do with that prison break? That's ridiculous."

Holy fuck. Vince froze, his gaze meeting Zara's. The army was here.

Glancing around the room for a place to hide, he quietly pulled her off the counter and set her back on her feet. The cupboards were too small and there weren't any closets. The break room door stood ajar. Wordlessly, he pointed behind it.

She nodded.

He followed her, taking care not to hit the door. From where Rand and the army people were standing, they'd be able to see if the door moved. And that wouldn't be good. He pressed her against the wall, caging her between his arms.

Here he was, putting Zara in grave danger again.

She leaned in until her lips grazed his ear. "I'll cloak us."

He gave a brusque nod, cursing to himself that yet again, *he* wasn't the one protecting *her*. Almost immediately, energy skated over his skin and he could tell they were invisible.

"There's no need to get hostile," the woman was saying to Rand.

"I'm not—"

"Are you refusing to cooperate with Army Intelligence?" It was the man.

"AIU will not be happy," the woman said with a sniff. Vince imagined her looking down her nose at Rand.

Before Rand could answer, the door to the garage opened again.

"'Scuse me." It sounded like Shane, one of the technicians. Heavy footsteps came down the hall and stopped just outside the break room.

Vince willed the man not to push on the door. He and Zara may be cloaked, but they still had mass.

Shane took two steps inside and glanced round the room. He frowned, as if he'd expected to find them here. He grabbed a sports drink from the refrigerator and turned to go. The drawing pad on the table got his attention. Vince had been sketching a picture of Zara from behind. Shane closed the pad and put it on a stack of magazines near the couch, then strode toward the door. But instead of leaving, he stopped in the doorway and leaned against the doorjamb.

More footsteps. Rand and the army folks were coming closer.

"A colossal waste of my time," Rand muttered.

Vince peeked through the crack between the door and the frame. He saw Rand go into his office ahead of the two army assholes and give the room a quick glance. He must be looking to make sure Vince and Zara weren't there, Vince thought.

"Take a seat inside." He pointed into his office.

The woman went in and sat down, but just as the man was passing the break room door, the buzzer on Zara's cupcakes went off.

She jumped, hitting the door. It swung outward slightly.

Vince gripped her hand even tighter.

The man turned around and looked in this direction. Vince held his breath. Had he seen the door move?

"What's that?" The man's features reminded Vince of a rat's.

"I'm making cupcakes," Shane said, his tone cool and even. "I'd offer you one, but since we weren't expecting you, I didn't make enough."

CHAPTER EIGHT

*V*ince was going stir-crazy. If he sat still any longer, he was liable to implode. The break room at Reckless no longer smelled of cupcakes but of old coffee, cigarettes, and a tinge of BO—not his at least. He'd been showering twice, sometimes three times a day since he'd gotten here.

He stood and paced. Rand and two of his guys sat at the table, staring at a computer screen where a satellite image map was displayed.

"You're a fucking genius," Rand said to Vince.

He rubbed the back of his neck. "Yeah, well, save your accolades in case it turns out to be a bust."

Rand shook his head. "Not gonna happen. This is golden."

"You think?" Vince asked, hardly able to keep from grinning.

Rand swiveled in his chair, chewing on his toothpick. "Listen. With the army essentially working two fronts right now—the manhunt for you, which, by the way, got a little too close for comfort this afternoon —and the current skirmish with the Iron Guild, they're stretched to the limits of their resources. Trust me. I've done this a time or two. They're not going to be expecting a heist in their own backyard by a couple of hoodlums."

"Watch who you're calling a hoodlum," Shane shot back, running a hand through his unruly black hair.

"Yeah," said Arlo. "What we do takes skill, finesse, precision."

"Equipment extraction engineers? Is that better?" Rand moved the toothpick from one side of his cheek to the other.

Shane laced his tattooed fingers together behind his head. "Much better."

"Just call us the Triple E's."

"Sounds like the name of a dude ranch," Rand said.

"If that ranch had steel horses named Harley and Davidson," Shane said with a snort. "Get it?"

Arlo rolled his eyes. "Someone get me some melted butter to go with the corn."

In addition to the legit business of Reckless Motor Sports and the adjacent off-road park that hosted sanctioned motocross events, Rand also operated an illegal chop shop, which sold army vehicles and equipment on the black market. When Vince learned of this, he told them about a huge army facility located a few miles from the Institute where surplus heavy equipment, maintenance vans and VIP vehicles were stored. The prisoners passed it every day on the way to the railroad job site.

Rand had wasted no time in pulling up a satellite image of the area.

"When do you think you'll check it out?" Vince asked.

The three men looked at each other. Arlo held out his hand to defer to Rand. "Ask the boss."

Rand thought for a moment. "Soon."

"I say tonight," said Shane. "Strike while the iron is hot."

Rand looked at Arlo. "You down with that?"

The guy nodded. "Sounds like a good way to spend a Friday night. Eating pizza and stealing from the army."

"Tonight it is then," Rand said.

Vince ground to a halt. "I'm going with you."

The three men cranked around in their chairs.

Shane looked confused. "You're shitting me, right? Didn't you just get out of the joint?"

"Yeah, but I can drive you straight there. Point out the side door that's hard to see from the road."

"Hell," Shane said. "When I got out of the big house, I slept for a week."

According to Rand, many of the men who worked

for him had past run-ins with the Pacifican army, some more serious than others. They all had chips on their shoulders when it came to the army, which explained Shane's reaction earlier when he'd covered for Vince and Zara.

After the AIU agents had left, Vince felt as if he'd been hit by a tidal wave. Not only had his presence put Zara in grave danger, he'd been unable to do anything to protect her.

What a fucking inadequate excuse for a man.

Rand pushed his chair from the table and stood. "Can you two gentlemen give us a minute?"

Vince had a feeling he wasn't going to like this.

Shane and Arlo got up and shuffled out into the garage. The metal door banged shut behind them.

Rand poured himself a cup of coffee, added two mounded spoonfuls of sugar and a trickle of cream, and began to stir vigorously. The *tink tink* sound grated on Vince's nerves.

"Listen," he said. "I know you're eager to participate, and I can respect that, but it's too soon. Based on that little visit from AIU, they're still hot on your tail."

Screw those AIU bastards. "You said yourself that this was going to be easy. Besides, this is my intel."

Rand gave a dismissive wave of his hand. "There will be a finder's fee for you, regardless. And if our take is as good as I think it will be, you should be pretty happy with it."

He wasn't about to be railroaded. "I don't care about the damn money," he said, pounding his fist on the table. "I want to go. This is something—"

"Give it time, man." Rand took a sip of his coffee, clearly unfazed by Vince's anger. "Get reacquainted with your life. Enjoy yourself. There will be plenty of other opportunities. I get it. Trust me."

Vince paced the length of the small room. "No, you don't. Once your men hit the storage facility, the army will lock things down tight. It's a chance for me to stick it to them before that happens and say *screw you*."

"But you stuck it to them when you escaped. Isn't that enough for now?"

Vince was so frustrated that he wanted to lash out at something. Punch the wall. Kick over the table.

"The escape plan wasn't my doing. I tried to get out of that place many times over the years and failed. When Zara showed up, I was just along for the ride, reacting to the events around me. I didn't take charge and make it happen. This raid, however, and the havoc it will cause will be because of *me*."

Rand nodded. "Revenge is a powerful motivator, but is now the best time for that? Shouldn't you be focused on what's in front of you rather than what's behind you?"

Vince cursed under his breath and continued pacing. Since he'd arrived, he'd been having a hard time sleeping. He was irritable, hadn't had much of an appetite. Hell, he'd even turned down a blow job in the shower that first night. Who the hell did that?

"Don't you get it? I can't move forward until I've righted some wrongs in my past. And here's a chance for me to do just that."

Rand blew out a long breath as he turned his mug around so that the handle was facing the opposite direction. A muscle in his jaw ticked. When he lifted his gaze, Vince could tell he'd made up his mind.

"Okay, fine," he said. "I'll let 'em know you'll be coming."

———

ZARA DIDN'T WANT to be one of *those* women. The kind who nagged her man, ordered him around and worried about him as if he were her child. *That's way too much salt. It's not good for you. Did you take out the trash? What time are you going to be home? Careful, you'll burn yourself.*

This was Vince's life, she told herself, not hers. He could make his own decisions, right?

Rubbing her forehead, she felt a headache starting to form. "You just got out of prison, and you're going on a raid? That makes no sense, Vince. The army is still looking for you."

If it hadn't been for those two AIU agents showing up when they had, she and Vince would've probably spent the rest of the afternoon in bed, making love and getting reacquainted with each other. She'd thought she was getting through to him—he'd finally asked about Darius and wanted to know all about his son—and then everything went back to the way it was before.

Vince stood at the foot of the bed, arms crossed, an angry look on his face. "You expect me to sit around and do nothing. Jesus, Zara, if you remember anything about me, you know I can't do that. It's not who I am."

His comment stung. He was putting distance between them that she wasn't sure she'd be able to overcome.

"And I don't expect you to," she said. "It just seems crazy to go back to that place right now. Things are too hot. Why do you need to do this now?" What she didn't say was, *before you even meet our son,* but she had a pretty good idea that Vince knew what she was implying.

He ran a hand over his buzz cut, and for a moment she thought he might change his mind, climb into the bed with her and tell her he wasn't going. But he didn't.

"This is something I need to do."

———

THE WAREHOUSE DISTRICT on Old Smokey Point Way looked like a ghost town. Several pieces of trash tumbleweeded across the quiet road. Tall grass grew from cracks in the asphalt parking lots.

Vince stretched his cramped muscles. For over an

hour, he'd been cooped up in a storage compartment hidden beneath the floor of the van. Even though Arlo had been able to avoid all the roadblocks, they didn't want to take any chances that they'd be pulled over and asked to produce their papers. According to Rand, getting a fake ID was easy enough, but that could take several weeks. Vince didn't want to wait and miss out on this opportunity for revenge against the system that had taken so much from him. Besides, this was his intel. He deserved to be here.

Shane peered out the windshield from the passenger seat. "Welcome to the thriving metropolis of Where-The-Hell-Are-We."

"The pride of the Pacifican army," Arlo quipped.

To the left was a nearby Dumpster overflowing with garbage. An awning over one of the doors hung at an angle.

"And it's not much better in the daytime," Vince said. "I don't think I once saw another vehicle on this road." He pointed to the right where several low-lying warehouses were surrounded by a chain link fence. "That's the back of the facility there. The main entrance is on the other side."

They drove around the corner and backed into an alley across the street, taking care not to hit the dented green Dumpster. The plan was to get inside and scope out the place first. Then, if there was anything of value,

Shane would go back for the van, they'd load it quickly and get the hell out.

Pulling down their black facemasks, the three men exited the vehicle and jogged in tandem to the mouth of the alley.

"And you've only seen guards during business hours?" Arlo asked, confirming what Vince had told them earlier.

He nodded. "During the day, yes, there was someone at the gate, but when the prison transport drove past in the evening, the place always looked completely dead. Like it does now. Doesn't mean there aren't any guards milling around somewhere."

Shane pointed to the Dumpster at the mouth of the alley. "We'll wait here for a few minutes. See if we spot anyone. If not, we'll go in."

Vince leaned against the brick wall and crossed his arms. He scanned the facility's parking lot, looking for movement, but the night was calm. A dog barked in the distance and a light breeze blew through the surrounding trees. If Vince were to climb to the top of one of them, he would probably be able to see the lights of the south guard tower at the Institute. The thought made his stomach clench. Having that hellhole so close made him even more determined to succeed tonight. It was going to be so satisfying to stick it to them right under their goddamn noses.

As they waited, Shane and Arlo talked in hushed

tones about an upcoming motocross event at Reckless. Shane had a boy who was going to compete for the first time. Vince found it curious that these two were criminals by night and regular dudes by day. In a way, just like Zara was. He wondered how long it would take to find his own place in this world.

It killed him to think about his conversation with her. She'd had tears in her eyes as she tried to talk him out of going. He'd wanted to drag her into his arms, soothe away her fears, but he knew that the moment he did, he would have caved. He would do anything to make her happy—except agree not to go on this raid. She'd have to accept that this was something he had to do.

"Ready, gents?" Shane said, jerking Vince from his thoughts.

Arlo motioned his head in the direction of the streetlamp. "You going to take care of that?"

"Guess I'm going to have to." Shane pulled a gun from his pocket, screwed on a silencer, and took aim at the streetlight. The first shot missed completely. The second one ricocheted off the pole with a loud metallic ping.

Arlo cursed under his breath. "Does someone need their eyes checked?"

Shane's expression said he wasn't amused. "If the marksman in this group hadn't broken his wrist doing yoga, this wouldn't be an issue."

Vince glanced over and noticed for the first time a black cast peeking out from under Arlo's sleeve.

"For your information, I didn't break it doing yoga. It was Pilates."

"My bad." Shane rolled his eyes. "Big difference."

"It is, but whatever. A really hot chick at the gym was having problems with one of the machines. I tried to help her, it slipped, and this happened. But it's all good. She felt terrible. Made it up to me later." He grinned.

Shane raised a brow. "One night in the sack is worth being incapacitated for weeks?"

"For the record, it's been more than just one night."

Vince was getting impatient. They needed to get this show on the road. "Let me try."

Shane handed him the gun. "Be my guest."

He held it in his hands to get a feel for how the weight was distributed and thought about the last time he'd fired a gun. It had been with his father at the shooting range on Abbott Street. Vince had done so well that day that he'd gotten his picture taken. He wondered if it was still posted on their wall.

He took aim at the streetlight and fired. It popped and the place went dark.

"Nice work," Arlo said. "You can do all the shooting from now on."

He gave Shane back the gun, and they jogged across the street.

The gate consisted of two chain link sections

padlocked together. The sign in front read: Army Surplus. Deliveries Only. Keep Out.

Several small, hunching shadows, one larger than the others, ambled across the road in front of them. Raccoons. They slipped through a break in the fence.

Shane held up a pair of wire cutters and snipped the air. "Maybe I won't be needing these after all."

Vince and the men headed over to the break. It wasn't big enough, so they did have to make a few more cuts. After they squeezed through, Vince pointed to the first building. "There's the entrance. Next to that delivery bay."

Before they'd taken more than a few steps, Arlo grabbed their collars. "Stop," he growled, jerking his chin toward a security camera on a tall pole.

He threw a rock to see if it was motion sensitive. It didn't move.

"I'm not sure that it's even on," Arlo said, "But we need to assume it is. Vince, think you can hit that as well?"

"Yep." He took the gun from Shane, and with one shot, he took out the camera.

Vince's ego swelled when he caught the two men giving each other a look that said they were impressed as hell.

Shane picked the lock and soon they were inside, snapping on their flashlights. Numerous rows of wooden crates were stacked fifteen or twenty feet high.

Arlo peeked inside a few of them. Munitions and firearms. Bingo.

On the far side were items too big for crates. Dozens of work trucks and vehicles, including four brand new Mercedes, still with plastic on the windshields to protect the glass.

Shane peered inside one of them. "Yes!" he said, rubbing his hands together. "The keys are in the ignition. Once the numbers are filed off, they'll fetch a handsome price. Too bad we can't take them all."

Vince remembered driving past this facility in the prison transport as these cars were being offloaded from the semi-trailer. Keetch had wondered what army VIPs were going to be driving them.

Vince smiled now, hoping that the roadblocks had delayed their delivery.

On the side window of each car was a sticker with the name and address of whom it belonged to. A colonel in Lakemont. A high-ranking official in Hunt's Point. A commander in downtown New Seattle. Vince's gut burned when he saw the name on the first car.

A Dr. Uri Dobrynin with an address in Brewster Park.

Pay dirt. He tore off the paper and shoved it into his pocket.

"We'll load a Merc and see what else we can fit," Arlo said, chewing more furiously on his gum. "Shane, go get the van."

He'd only been gone for a minute when Arlo's comm device beeped.

"We've got trouble." Shane's tone was urgent. "Two guards are approaching your location in a golf cart."

Arlo cursed. "Have they seen you?"

"I don't think so," Shane whispered. "I just got back to the alley."

"Good. Stay put for now."

Vince clenched his fists. He didn't care what he needed to do; there was no way in hell he was going to get caught.

He followed Arlo down a row of pallets and crouched so they had a clear view of the door they'd come through.

Arlo cupped the comm device to shield his voice. "Where are they now? Can you see them?"

"Parking the golf cart in front of the delivery bay." There was a pause. "And now they're walking toward the door we came in."

"Walking?" Vince asked, confused. "They'd be running if they thought they had a break in."

"Agreed," Arlo replied.

Maybe they were investigating the lack of a video feed.

Vince glanced at the door. Damn. It was unlocked. He couldn't remember if the latch was visible on the outside or if it was just a keyhole. Sprinting over there, he held his breath and turned the deadbolt as quietly as possible. It made a faint but very distinctive click.

The sound of muffled voices could be heard through the steel door, and he thought he heard the word *broken*.

A moment later the door handle jiggled. Vince's heart banged in his chest. The lock held.

Arlo tapped his temple. "Good thinking," he mouthed. "But let's get out of here. They'll never know we were here."

"Without taking anything?" Vince glanced at Dr. Dobrynin's soon-to-be-delivered new car.

"We'll come back another time, my friend. We must be patient and not do anything stupid."

But he couldn't just walk away. It was like candy to a sugar-starved diabetic. No matter how much he tried to talk himself out of it, tell himself it was a fool's errand, he couldn't leave without the car.

"Open the south delivery bay on your way out," he told Arlo. "And the gate at the back."

The other man turned, flipping his hair out of his face. "What the hell?"

"I'm getting even with an old friend. Remember the elementary school we passed on Old Smokey Point Way?"

"Yes, but—"

A key sounded in the lock. They were officially out of time.

"Meet you behind the portables in ten. And have the van ready."

"You're a fucking lunatic, bro," Arlo said, shaking his head, "but I like your style." Then the guy spun on his heel and beelined for the south entrance.

Vince peeled off the plastic from the windshield of the doctor's car just as the guards entered the warehouse. He carefully opened the door and slipped into the driver's seat.

With his hand on the ignition, he thought about what Arlo had said. It was true. No one had ever accused him of being sane.

CHAPTER NINE

"*H*e did *what?*" Zara wasn't sure whether to laugh like everyone else or scream out her frustration.

Vince had been a hair's breadth from getting captured again. What was he thinking?

Then she thought about what Mariah had said about being patient and she took a deep breath. But how could she be patient when his actions were so...so reckless? She balled her hands into fists and crossed her arms in front of her.

A beautiful Mercedes sedan was parked in the last bay of the garage. Rand was walking around it and nodding appreciatively. "I'd have paid big bucks for a drone's eye view of how it all went down."

"Me, too," Shane chimed in.

Zara was confused. "But you were there, weren't you?"

"Yeah, but not *there* there, you know? After leaving the warehouse, we drove the van to a nearby school and waited for, like, five minutes when—"

"No, *you* did that," Arlo said. "I opened the garage, the chain link gate, and then ran like hell."

Shane rolled his eyes. "Okay, fine. As I was saying, all of a sudden there's a flash of black coming around the corner, a screech of brakes, and boom, Vince pulls up in *this* car. He drives it up into the van, shuts the door and here we are."

"Jay-zus," Rand said.

"Yeah, I'm telling you," said Shane, holding his hands up like a maestro, "it was *Grand Theft Auto* meets *The Fast and the Furious*."

Vince looked like a cat who had just swallowed a canary. Unable to keep from smiling, he took a swig of beer and ended up spilling half of it down the front of him. He was clearly avoiding her gaze, probably because then he'd have to deal with her feelings about his reckless behavior. It was easier for him if he just kept drinking.

"Thank God you drive better than you drink." Arlo threw him a clean rag from a nearby workbench.

"Just call me Vin. Vin Diesel." Vince dabbed his T-shirt.

Arlo gave Rand a pointed look and lowered his voice,

but not low enough that Zara couldn't hear. "I'm telling you, the guy was incredible. Smart. Good instincts. Fearless as hell. You could really use another guy with Cooper gone...unless you think Coop is coming back."

Rand shrugged. "Hard to say."

Holy crap, Zara thought, rubbing her eyes. They wanted Vince to come work for them? She tried not to think of the danger he'd be exposed to on a regular basis.

Rand tossed a thick envelope to Vince.

"What's this?" he asked.

"Open it."

Vince did. Inside was a thick stack of money. "What's it for?"

Rand jutted his chin at the car. "Your cut. Told you it would be good."

"So soon?" Vince frowned. "But the car just got here."

"I've got a buyer already. Someone I've done business with before. Wants it sight unseen. Normally, my guys get paid when I get paid, but I figured you could use the money now. And I...uh...wasn't sure what your plans were."

Zara held her breath. She wasn't sure what Vince's plans were either.

Vince tucked the envelope into his back pocket. "Thanks."

Rand held out his hand. "The job's yours if you want it."

"I appreciate that," Vince said, his smile wider now as he shook Rand's hand.

Her heart sank. It didn't sound as if she and Darius were part of his plans. Without anyone noticing, she slipped from the garage and went back to the small apartment to pack her things.

―――――――――

WHERE THE HELL WAS ZARA? He wanted to share his excitement with her.

Blood raced through Vince's veins as he took the stairs to the apartment two at a time. He hadn't felt this damn good in a long time.

Not only was he a free man and had, in a small way, successfully thwarted the army, he'd also made a wad of cash, gotten accolades from the guys *and* obtained the doctor's home address.

He wasn't going to do anything with the information now, but he had it and could kick that ball into motion when the time was right.

A dream without the means to achieve it was like an empty gun. Until it was loaded, it was just a useless lump of steel weighing you down.

He was finally, *finally* taking control of his life again. It felt fucking great, and he wanted to share it with Zara.

He'd looked for her down in the garage but she wasn't there. She'd probably gotten tired of the banter between half-drunk men who were slapping each other on the back for a job well done. She wasn't in the break room either, so he figured she'd gone back to the apartment. Spotting a plate of her cupcakes, he'd grabbed one on the way out and shoved it in his mouth.

But his good mood vanished the moment he opened the door.

Zara was there all right. On the bed.

But she appeared to be packing.

He shut the apartment door behind him with a bang. "What are you doing?"

She jumped, but didn't look up at him. "Just putting my things together," she said quietly, seemingly unaffected by his bold entrance.

"Why?" he said, his tone harsher than he intended.

"As soon as the roadblocks are lifted, I'll be able to head home."

I, not *we*.

He stormed over to the bed in three long strides, rattling a few things on the nightstand. "When were you planning to discuss this with me?"

"What's there to discuss? I have responsibilities. I need to get back to Darius and to work." She continued folding clothes and putting them into her duffel bag.

He ran a hand over his buzz cut as a war of emotions clanged around in his head. So she was just going to leave him here? That was it? No discussion. No making plans. No nothing.

"And what about me?" The minute he uttered the words, he realized how pathetic and selfish he sounded, but he didn't care. He didn't want her to go, but didn't know what to say to change her mind.

Her brow lifted. "You seem to be doing fine. You've got a place to stay. You've got friends. A job. I'm happy for you, Vince. I really am."

He looked at the room and thought about being here by himself without her. The walls would close in around him. The shadows would intensify. It would be unbearable. She'd been a calming presence, helping to keep him grounded and sane. A light in his dark world. He wasn't ready for her to leave. Without her, he would...

No. He was not *fine* with this. Not one fucking bit.

He swept her duffel from the bed, scattering her newly folded clothes over the floor.

"What the hell, Vince!"

The anger inside him raged on, and the blank wall next to the bed drew his attention. "So you're leaving the first chance you get?"

"And that bothers you?"

"Hell yeah, it bothers me," he said and punched his fist through the drywall.

"Vince! Oh my God!" She clamped a hand over her mouth. "What is *wrong* with you?"

He paced along the edge of the bed, rubbing his sore

hand, restless as a jungle cat. "For your information, I haven't taken the job."

"Well, it sure sounded like you had." The indignation in her tone was unmistakable as she slipped off the bed, brushed past him and began to pick up the clothes from the floor.

So that was it, huh? She was pissed about what he might be doing and didn't want to stick around. "That's a little like the pot calling the kettle black, wouldn't you say?"

"What are you talking about?"

"You're mad because you think I'm going to be stealing cars for a living. That the ex-con slash ex-boyfriend is really just a common criminal, when you, yourself, are a thief." He stood, towering over her, his arms crossed over his chest. "Don't you think that's the least bit hypocritical?"

"No," she said vehemently. "That's not it at all."

He didn't believe her. "For your information, I *was* going to discuss it with you first. Unlike what you're doing now."

She jumped to her feet, dark eyes flashing with her own rage. "Don't you dare pull that on me, Vince Crawford," she said, poking him in the chest. "You've kept me at arm's length ever since we arrived. You've barely asked about our son. What was I supposed to think?"

"I have not."

"Yes, you have." She spun on her heel, clearly disgusted with him, and grabbed a sock from the floor. "You hardly talk to me. You won't touch me. Hell, you won't even eat any of my damn cupcakes."

"You're mad at me because I didn't eat a cupcake?"

She made a sound of frustration. "Not just because of a cupcake, but that's part of it, yes. There was a time when you used to love the food I made for you."

"You're mad because of a cupcake," he repeated softly, feeling a smile twitching at the corners of his mouth.

"*Hello?* It's called a sign of affection. And you rebuffed it. Just like you did with all my other attempts." She was shoving things into her bag faster now, and without folding them. "I hope you know how to do drywall work, because Asher is going to be pissed."

Yeah, well, Asher could go fuck himself.

He grasped her hands and pulled her to her feet, all of his earlier anger gone. "I don't want you to leave, Zara. I don't want you to be apart from me."

"Why? Because then you won't have anyone you can actively ignore?" Her lips remained parted and her breasts rose and fell as she huffed out a breath.

"Because I care about you. And...and I want to be with you."

"Get a dog."

"I'm serious, Zara. I want you to stay with me." He

brushed a strand of hair from her face, and her expression softened.

God, she was beautiful, her skin so smooth and flawless, her eyes framed with impossibly thick lashes. And she smelled incredible. A mixture of soap and something enticingly sweet.

She started to say something, probably another protest. She'd used baked goods and animals already. Who knew what else she was going to try?

To silence her, he hauled her close and captured her mouth with his. Her lips were soft and he pushed his tongue inside, feeling as if he could devour her.

She let out a little moan that went straight to his groin.

Enough with this.

His patience was gone.

Cupping his palms under her butt, he scooped her up, wrapped her legs around his waist, and carried her to the bed. The friction of her grinding against him made him even harder. They tumbled to the mattress in a single mass, and their clothes went flying.

His erection jutted out at her, a bead of liquid balanced on the tip.

From somewhere, she produced a condom and handed it to him. He turned the latex disc over in his hand. Damn it. How did this thing work?

They'd only ever had sex in Cascadia, where they didn't have modern conveniences like birth control, so he hadn't used one before. He did try to take a box of condoms through the portal once, but it had disintegrated just like he thought it would by the time he got to the other side.

"Here. Like this," she said, flipping it over and placing it on the head of his penis. Her touch was as light as a butterfly. "Now, just roll it down."

Seeing her do it would be much more interesting, he decided. "No. You." When she didn't move fast enough, he grabbed her hands and positioned them on his shaft. She wrapped her fingers around him tentatively, then the tip of her tongue darted out as she sheathed him in latex.

He imagined it'd be pretty damn interesting to see her mouth around him too...but that could wait.

"Green?" he asked when she was done.

She smiled sheepishly. "That's all they had in the bathroom downstairs."

"I look like a carnival balloon."

"But twice the fun."

"Twice?" He grasped her thighs and roughly repositioned her beneath him, making her creamy breasts bounce.

She giggled. "Okay, three times."

He lifted her hips and her knees fell open, exposing her sex to him. He gently rolled her beaded nipple with one hand, producing a soft moan from her lips, while the other hand parted her pink folds and slipped a finger inside.

"God, Zara. You're already so wet." And when he rolled that tiny bundle of flesh between his finger and thumb, pressing a little bit harder, she writhed with pleasure.

"Oh Vince," she cried out, holding his hand in place and moving restlessly against him. "I missed you so much. I missed...this."

"Me, too." He felt a surge of male pride that he could please her so easily with just one touch.

Gripping the base of his cock, veins visible through the colored latex, he pushed inside her with one powerful thrust. It took every ounce of willpower he possessed to remain still for a moment, giving her a chance to adjust to his thick girth. He reveled in the incredible sensation of being cocooned inside her body, her legs around his waist and her soft, lush breasts pressed to his chest.

It had been ten long years since they'd been together like this. But even as he'd lain on a cot in his cell, reliving every exquisite memory, the sex hadn't been a fraction as hot as this.

He groaned loudly as he began to piston his hips.

"You feel...so good," he growled against her neck, his face buried in her luxurious hair. He knew he wasn't going to last long.

Cool hands slipped up and down his back and she matched his rhythm. "So do you."

His mouth found hers again, and the pressure in his balls intensified.

Vince berated himself for waiting so long to make love with Zara. They could've been doing this every day and every night since he'd gotten out. Hell, he could've gotten a blow job in the shower fifteen minutes after arriving if he hadn't been so messed up.

They had so much lost time to make up for. He hoped he'd convinced her to stay, at least a little while longer.

Her internal muscles pulsed and squeezed him, signaling her impending release.

Vince roared as a powerful orgasm slammed through his own body, pumping out his seed in several long bursts.

When it was over, he collapsed on top of her without pulling out, taking care not to crush her with his body weight.

A thin layer of sweat covered both of them and the musky scent of their lovemaking filled the air.

"You lied to me, Vince," she said softly in his ear.

Pushing up on his elbows, he looked down at her face. Her raven hair was splayed out across the pillow, her lips were flushed and swollen, and her cheeks had that rosy I-just-had-sex glow.

Holy hell, she was ravishing.

"What are you talking about?"

"You told me you didn't want a cupcake."

"Excuse me?"

She nibbled on his lip, drawing it between her teeth. "But from what I taste, I can tell that you've already had one."

ZARA WOKE TO A FEATHERLIKE, almost ticklish sensation on her belly, and she became aware of a solid wall of heat pressed against her from behind.

Vince. He was spooning her, his broad hand gently rubbing her stomach.

She couldn't believe he was still here. She'd grown used to waking up and finding him gone.

"Hey," he said, his voice low and rumbly.

She yawned. "What time is it?"

He swept her hair from her shoulder and kissed her neck. "It's still early."

The intimate details of their marathon lovemaking session flooded her mind. If she counted correctly, she'd had at least four pretty mind-blowing orgasms.

His hand slipped lower, confidently skimming her body as if it were his own, and delved into her moist cleft.

"Vince!" She gasped at his boldness.

The hard length of his erection pressed into her backside, a clear indicator of his intention.

"I probably can't do it again so soon," she said.

His mouth quirked. "After last night, you have doubts that I can satisfy you?"

"For one thing, we don't have any more condoms."

"Easily solved," he murmured huskily. "I'll run to the men's bathroom in the garage and get a few more from the vending machine. What color do you want—or should I surprise you?"

She shouldn't be surprised at his willingness to do whatever it took. Going a decade without sex had to make you a little crazy.

"I'm...ah...a little sore down there. I'm going to need a little time. Is that okay?"

His hand stilled. "I hurt you?"

She rolled to her back and looked up at his face. His brows were two dark slashes of concern on his forehead.

"It's not that," she said, reaching up to stroke his jaw. "It's just that...well, I'm not used to having so much sex in such a short period of time."

He was silent for a moment as he considered what she'd said. "Would my tongue hurt?"

A thrill ran down her spine, but then she thought about that first night in the shower. "No, it wouldn't hurt. Not at all. But let me put my mouth on you first."

"No."

She was confused. Didn't all men love it? "Why not?"

"We can do it at the same time."

And before she could put two and two together, he pulled her on top of him so that she was straddling his face; his thick, heavy erection lay on his belly in front of her.

Whoa.

Strong fingers gripped her thighs and his thumbs gently opened her folds. One flick of his tongue had her shuddering from head to toe.

She slipped her mouth over the broad head of his penis and took him in as far as she could. He groaned beneath her, his voice vibrating over her most sensitive parts.

Her toes curled as intense pleasure quickly spiraled through her, but the sensation was almost too much. She tried to arch her hips away from him to get a reprieve, but his iron grip kept her rooted in place. She'd have cried out if she could have, so instead she sucked on him harder.

A vicious curse escaped his lips. "Zara...I'm... almost...there." Now it was his turn to try to pull away from her.

Nope. Not going to happen.

She tapped his thigh to let him know it was okay to release into her mouth.

His shaft pulsed and he nearly roared, spurting hot seed in the back of her throat. When they were done, she fell next to him on the pillow, her whole body like mush, the juncture between her thighs still tingling.

"You okay?" she asked.

"I'm—that was— Yeah. Doing well."

Yep. That about summed it up for her, too.

With her arm flung over her face, her heart rate slowly returned to normal. Vince snored and rolled to his side.

Was he finally worn out? Maybe five times was the charm. An oral sex *coup de grace*.

She couldn't get over how volatile he was. Cold as ice one moment, then attentive as hell the next. The silvery scars crisscrossing his back drew her attention again, reminding her of the pain and suffering he'd endured. Reaching out, she gingerly ran her fingertips over the raised flesh.

He'd been infuriated at the thought that she might be leaving, but the fact of the matter was, she couldn't stay here forever. She had a life beyond Reckless. A job that paid the bills. A son she desperately missed.

Even though she was still euphoric over making love with Vince after all this time, it was tempered by disappointment that he still hadn't mentioned Darius again. Wouldn't a man be eager to meet the boy he'd fathered?

Vince had been right about one thing. They couldn't just start up where they'd left off. They were two different people now. His time in prison had obviously changed him. She was a mother, and her first priority had to be her son. She couldn't sit around, waiting and hoping that Vince would figure things out. And when he did, she couldn't assume that she and Darius would be included.

The old Zara could have waited—the young, idealistic Zara with no real responsibilities. But the new Zara couldn't.

If he had no interest in being a father to their son, then a relationship with him would be next to impossible, no matter how much she still wanted him.

CHAPTER TEN

A single headlight cut a swath through the darkness as Vince drove the Harley onto a quiet street.

The day after the raid had been uneventful. He'd done some more gravel work with the backhoe and Zara had helped Rand's office manager with some project.

Guilt pricked at his conscience that he was again doing something that she would not want him to do.

The houses in this part of New Seattle were few and far between with long driveways that disappeared into the woods. You could only see a few of them from the road, and of those, several had old cars parked out front on overgrown lawns. It was the kind of place where people minded their own business and didn't give a shit what their neighbors were doing.

He parked the borrowed bike near a clump of blackberry bushes and jogged down a narrow path that wound into the trees. If his research was correct, this should lead to a small trailer park on the edge of the Sammamish Slough, a slow-moving channel that joined Lake Sammamish and Lake Washington.

But more importantly, about a quarter of a mile downstream from the trailer park was a private golf course. And on the fourteenth hole, overlooking the sand trap, was a stately mansion that just happened to be owned by Dr. Uri Dobrynin.

Vince picked up the pace, knowing that every step was bringing him closer to the justice he craved.

His backpack was heavy and he had to reposition it every few steps. When he emerged from the trees a few minutes later, immediately to his left was a weathered sign that welcomed him to the Lakeshore Mobile Home Park.

Yes, just as he had hoped.

A yappy dog barked as he hurried between two trailers and headed for the water. His backpack hit a wind chime that clanged loudly, and he cringed.

Who hangs those things so low?

He waited, trying to figure out what to say if someone were to come outside and find him here. Dressed in all black with a dark backpack, he didn't exactly look as though he belonged. But when no one came out, he continued on his way.

Below the bulkhead on the slough were a dozen or so small docks for the residents. Vince took a quick scan and found what he was looking for. A small metal rowboat was tied to one of them.

Bingo.

He jumped from the bulkhead and in four steps he was at the end of the dock. The boat's lines were waterlogged and covered in moss from disuse, which was making them hard to untie. Screw it. He'd have to cut them. He'd just severed the first one when the nearest trailer's porch light came on.

Damn it. He was a sitting duck out here.

Climbing into the tippy boat, he crouched between the metal seats where it smelled of dead fish and hoped that anyone looking out would not be able to see him.

A rapid series of high-pitched barks filled the air. Raising his head a few inches, Vince saw a small white dog on the bulkhead looking in his direction.

Oh great.

He'd never been a fan of little dogs, and he sure as hell wasn't becoming one now.

"Pinkie," a woman shouted. "Get back in here."

Surprise. The dog kept barking. Only it was more frenzied now. Great.

The woman yelled again and when the dog continued to ignore her, she marched out in her robe and slippers and scooped him up. But instead of turning around and heading back to her trailer, she paused at the bulkhead. "What do you see?"

Vince's stomach clenched. If only he had Zara's cloaking talent and could make himself invisible, then the dog could bark his head off all he wanted.

The woman looked out over the canal. "Aw, heck. I can't see a thing without my glasses." He let out a long, controlled breath, immensely grateful for old women and poor eyesight. "Did you see a rat?"

Vince's eyes widened and his heart lodged in his throat. A rat? He scanned the bottom of the boat looking for movement of any kind. Skin-covered tails. Beady black eyes.

He didn't see anything, but that didn't mean they weren't around somewhere. If he were to choose, he'd rather live with a dozen tiny dogs—no, a hundred—than one single caged rat. He'd seen plenty while living in that filthy prison and had never gotten used to them. A fellow inmate had even woken to find one gnawing on his ear.

Water lapped against the side of the boat in a slightly different rhythm than before. Untethered at one end, it was drifting straight toward a jet ski tied to the next dock.

He glanced back at the woman. She was slowly mounting the steps of her trailer, the little dog tucked under her arm.

Come on, come on.

He didn't want to move until she was inside.

Five feet, four feet...

Damn. The jet ski was right there. Hitting it would make noise.

Screw it. He reached for the rope to pull the boat back in just as the woman's screen door banged shut.

After doing a quick rat check, he cut the second rope and quietly rowed downstream.

Ten minutes later, Vince was crouched in the dark behind a cluster of trees near the fourteenth hole, peering at Dr. Dobrynin's home through a pair of binoculars.

He smiled to himself. The backside was all windows to take advantage of the golf course view. And at night, it was the perfect fishbowl.

The expansive house was three stories tall with a daylight basement. A huge deck extended from the main floor and ran the length of the house. On the top floor, there was a small deck that he thought was called a widow's peak off one of the upstairs rooms. If he were to guess, he'd say that was the main bedroom.

It didn't take long for the doctor to come into view. Except for the day when Vince had been taken from his family and locked up in that godforsaken hellhole, this was the first time he'd seen the man outside the prison environment. He wore a dark blazer, an open-collared shirt, and a red ascot. If you glanced at it quickly, the splash of color at his neck looked like it could be blood.

Soon, it would be, Vince thought, fingering the eight-inch hunting knife at his waist. Rand had scores of firearms that Vince probably could've used, but he hadn't wanted to tell anyone his plans for fear that they'd try to talk him out of it.

Besides, he wanted to kill the bastard up close and see the light drain from his eyes.

As Vince watched, the doctor strode into what looked to be a formal dining room and sat at the head of the table. Several other people were seated around him. He cursed under his breath that the man wasn't alone, but no matter. He had all the time in the world and would lay in wait here until everyone left.

Vince hadn't known much about the doctor's personal life before, but since he was out of prison, he'd found a plethora of information online. Turned out, the man had lots of enemies and those enemies liked to talk. The tabloids were filled with the stuff. The government had tried to get some of the stuff erased, but they couldn't get to it all.

Married three times but currently single, the seventy-nine-year-old man had two grown children from whom he was estranged. Rumor had it that his first wife, the mother of his children, had left him because he had a fondness for young boys. His second wife, a former beauty queen, had died under mysterious circumstances, and his third wife divorced him after only one month.

Not exactly saint material. But then, Vince already knew that.

When the doctor lifted a champagne flute and smiled broadly at his guests, a white-hot heat surged through Vince, making it hard to see clearly. Ten years ago, from the back of a limousine where the man had sat with Vince, he'd ordered the execution of Vince's father. Vince had begged for his father's life, and when it became apparent that wasn't working, he'd lunged at the man only to be restrained by one of his bodyguards. Then, as a soldier took aim at his father and Vince screamed, the doctor had poured himself a glass of champagne and smiled.

Vince sat in the shadows near the mansion for several hours. By the time the last guest left, his arms and legs were stiff from sitting still so long. He stood and stretched, causing several vertebrae in his back to pop. He had to assume the doctor had a security system, so he needed to act fast before it was activated.

Palming a large knife, he sprinted across the manicured lawn, staying as low to the ground as possible. Thank God for the golf course and no fences, he thought as he flattened himself under the deck. The stairs were on the other side near the hot tub. He started to make his way over there when the French doors above him opened. He stopped abruptly.

Footsteps creaked overhead as one, maybe two people walked out onto the deck.

"Grandpa, have you ever made a hole in one?"

Vince froze. A child's voice. A boy. Possibly the same age as Darius.

"Yes, once, when I wasn't much older than you are now," Dr. Dobrynin replied.

Vince didn't understand it. He thought everyone had left. He hadn't seen any children at the party. Where had this boy come from?

"Mom said we're golfing in the morning. Is that true?"

"Yes, indeed," the doctor replied.

Vince's jaw clenched. The grandson wasn't leaving tonight.

The thought briefly crossed his mind that he could still carry out his plan. He could let himself into Dobrynin's bedroom and kill him while he slept.

But then there was the matter of the security system. And if he managed to get past that, what if the boy was the one who found him the next morning?

His thoughts flashed back to the day his father was killed. He'd never forgotten just how red the blood had looked as it dripped down the slight incline of their driveway. Seeing that had changed him forever and would haunt him 'til the day he died.

He didn't hear what the boy said next. All he knew was that he couldn't carry out his plan now.

CHAPTER ELEVEN

Zara woke the next morning with a start, but when she found Vince sound asleep beside her, she relaxed.

At nightfall, he'd borrowed one of Rand's motorcycles, said he was going out for a spin and that he would be gone for a while. She'd been worried sick about him, thinking maybe he'd been captured, but he came in around four in the morning and slipped into bed.

Without a word, he'd reached for her, making love to her slowly and tenderly, then fell asleep on his stomach with his arm draped across her belly.

She had no idea where he'd been, but it must have been exhausting.

Carefully extracting herself from under his arm, she grabbed her cell phone from the nightstand, and tiptoed into the bathroom. She shut the bathroom door quietly behind her and called home.

Olivia answered and assured her that everything was going well—except for the fact that Asher had ruined one of Zara's cupcake pans when he tried to fry an egg in it.

"An egg?"

"Yeah, don't ask."

When Darius came on the line, her arms ached with the need to hug him.

"When are you coming home, Mom?"

"Soon, honey. I really miss you. Hey, I hear school's going well. Are you having fun with Uncle Asher and Auntie Olivia?"

"Yeah, but Mom, did you forget about Conry?"

The dog clearly was a hit with Darius. "Has it been fun having him there, too?"

"He's been sleeping on my bed. I think he really likes me. Did you know that dogs love bacon?" He went on to tell her about a science project involving potions and an art project about bees. He was talking so fast she could barely keep up with him.

"Wow, that's so exciting. I can't wait for you to show me all of this in person. Hey, who's my favorite-ist person under the moon and stars?"

"You always ask me that," he said with an exasperated sigh.

"Yeah, then what's the answer?"

"I am."

She laughed. "Miss you, Squirt."

"I miss you, too, Mom. A billion times infinity."

After the call ended, she wiped the tears from her eyes and finished getting ready. Talking to her son only made her miss him more.

She gave her jeans on the counter a disdainful look. She'd been wearing them every day since they'd arrived and really wasn't thrilled to be putting them on again. If the roads didn't open up between here and home soon, she was going to have to do some shopping. But the more she thought about it, Vince could probably use a few things now.

Pulling her hair into a messy topknot, she decided to broach the subject with him about driving into town today. Even if they didn't shop for clothes, they did need a patch kit for the drywall. Emotions had been running high here at Reckless. Getting away for a few hours together might be good for both of them.

———

THE VINTAGE CLOTHING shop was located on Cole Street halfway between Griffin and Initial Avenue. Despite the weather, an elderly couple sat at a bistro table in front of the bakery next door, sipping coffee from paper cups and sharing an enormous cupcake. Zara smiled when the old man took a napkin and dabbed a crumb from the woman's chin. A snowplow rumbled past them on its way to the highway leading to the mountain pass. The roads were bare and slick in town, but at a slightly higher altitude, they'd be covered in snow.

Zara thought Vince was right behind her when she entered Second Time Around, but when she stopped at a rack of men's shirts, she realized he hadn't walked in yet.

He was glancing around the small shop, a wary expression on his face as if he were assessing how safe it was inside. When he caught her looking at him, he gave a thin-lipped smile and stepped through the door.

Part of her wanted go to him and ask if he was okay, but she decided not to address it so blatantly. These were all new sights and sounds for him. A much different environment than what he had been used to. He was bound to feel out of place and nervous about things at first. No need to draw attention to that fact. It was a victory in itself that he agreed to come into town with her at all.

"It'll be fun to get out," she'd said to him back at Reckless when she brought him a cup of coffee in bed. "No word on when they'll stop doing road checks, so we might as well make the best of it. Besides, we both could use a change of clothes. I'm getting tired of wearing my brother's old sweats and T-shirts."

The sheets were draped over his lower torso as he

sipped his coffee. "You don't think anyone will recognize me, do you?"

She looked at his buzz cut and his clean-shaven face. "Even if they show a picture of you on a Jumbo Tron, you look much different now. The new you could be one of the guys looking for the old you."

It was true. Ever since he cut his hair and shaved off his beard, he looked like a young army recruit. Except for his eyes. With a few wrinkles at the corners, they held the stark memories of ten long years spent behind bars.

The store had a mix of new and used clothes as well as a few toys and knickknacks. Not as extensive as the one in New Seattle where she'd bought the dress and shoes for the museum gala, but it wasn't bad.

In less than twenty minutes, she found three flannel shirts, two pairs of jeans and a leather coat for Vince, as well as several T-shirts, a pair of Rock n Republics and an oversized fisherman's knit sweater for her.

"All set?" she asked. Vince had his back to her and she couldn't figure out what he was looking at.

"I think you need to get these." He turned and held up the largest pair of granny panties that Zara had ever seen.

Laughter burst from her throat. "Oh my God, no way."

He held them off to the side, pinkie fingers up. "Are

you sure? They're kind of pretty with all these daisies. Our flower, you know."

She snatched them from him and tossed them back on the pile.

"As if." She snorted. "They'd come clear up to my chin." She spotted a doll on a nearby shelf. It was an iconic toy, but its name escaped her. "Who is this again?"

Vince gave her a pained expression. "Um, Ken?"

"Yeah, that's it." Not having grown up here, she couldn't remember. The girlfriend was Barbie. At least she knew that.

"Ken," she said, looking at the doll, "don't you think that underwear is disgusting? Yes, Zara," she said in a deep voice, "they are."

Without skipping a beat, Vince grabbed the Barbie from the shelf. "Personally," he said in falsetto, "I don't wear underwear."

She burst out laughing, then immediately clamped a hand over her mouth when she realized how loud she was. "You don't?" she asked in her Ken voice.

"No. I find them way too binding." Then Vince put the Barbie into her plastic convertible and rolled it toward Ken. "Hey big fella, I'll be back to pick you up later."

Zara didn't think she could laugh any harder until Vince grabbed Ken from her, pressed the two dolls together and stuck them both into the back seat of Barbie's car. She seriously almost peed her pants. An older woman looking through a tray of costume jewelry gave them the side-eye. The salesgirl behind the counter was trying not to smile.

"You are so naughty." She pushed him away from the dolls.

He grinned and let her back him up a few steps. "My sister used to make me play Barbies with her."

"Barbie and Ken getting married? Barbie and Ken going shopping?"

"Hardly. There'd be a break-in at Barbie's mansion. Naturally, Ken would go investigate. Then after he'd secured the premises and beat the crap out of the intruder, I'd shove Ken and Barbie into the same bed together, which would make my sister scream."

She punched him playfully in the chest. "How old were you?"

"Ten, maybe?" he said, grabbing her wrists and stopping the assault.

"So you've always been a control freak."

Without letting go, he moved her hands to the small of his back, pulling her to the hard plane of his chest, and stepped backward. She had no choice but to stutter-step with him. Her hip and upper thigh brushed against his groin—a sensation that was hard to ignore. Another step. Now his thigh was between hers, pressing against the crotch of her jeans.

"Barbie could've come to investigate with Ken if

she'd wanted to," he said, his warm breath ruffling her hair. "I wasn't stopping my sister."

"Maybe…maybe she could tell you'd have had a fit if she did."

"Or maybe she secretly liked it." A smile played at the corner of his mouth as he stopped moving backwards.

Such a smart ass. A crazy sexy smart ass that she wanted to kiss. Right here in the back of Second Time Around, between the men's shirts and the vintage purses.

"Why did she protest then?" she asked, her voice husky.

He shrugged. "I don't know. Why did she keep asking me to play? It's not like I hadn't done it every other time before."

Whiskey-colored eyes looked down at her, one brow slightly higher than the other as if he were challenging her to continue. He released her hands, but she kept them right where they were—pressed to the small of his back. Well, not exactly. She slipped them slightly lower to his tight, muscular ass.

With one finger, he lifted her chin. Something dark and delicious danced behind his eyes. "Don't have an answer?"

She stared at his lips and licked hers. "I'm not exactly thinking of children's games right now."

"That's good, Zara." His tone was low, confident and so overtly sexy that it made her panties wet. He turned her so that it was her back against the wall, not his. "Because neither am I."

Oh boy. They definitely weren't talking games anymore.

He braced a hand on the wall next to her and leaned in close, his other hand at his side, not touching her, all relaxed and casual-like. He gazed down at her, scanning her face as if he were seeing her for the first time.

Her lips heated, tingled, felt swollen in response to his scrutiny. She hoped she met his approval. He'd been so hard to decipher these past few days.

With his free hand, he threaded his fingers through her hair. His eyes were dark, intense. Dipping his head, he kissed her lightly on the mouth, then trailed his lips down her neck. Her whole body quivered in response, and her nipples tingled. But just as she was about to wrap her arms around his neck, he pulled away, leaving her wanting so much more.

Oh...that's right. A store. With people.

When they exited Second Time Around with their purchases, the smell of warm baked goods caused her to stop in the middle of the sidewalk.

"Are you hungry?" She looked longingly at the bakery with its forest green awning and neon cupcake sign in the window.

Nodding, he flashed a crooked grin her way. "I'm sure their stuff isn't half as good as yours, but yeah, I could eat something."

A few minutes later, they were sitting at a table by the window with two espressos and a cupcake to share, just like that older couple when they'd first walked by. The thought made her smile.

"So tell me about your work," Vince said, pulling the paper from the cupcake.

"At the library or with the sisters?"

"Both. And I want to know why you aren't working at a bakery. I thought that was your dream—to open up a bakery one day."

She thought about the kitchen back home. Her father, the big strong warrior, had taught her how to make bread. He'd take her shopping in the open-air market for supplies, then they'd come home and bake together. Her mother would sit at the kitchen table doing her needlepoint while her brother would be playing outside with his friends. It was a nice memory. Too bad it hadn't lasted. After her father was gone, she continued baking as a way to honor his memory. It soon became a part of who she was.

She glanced over the counter to the back of the bakery and looked wistfully at the industrial ovens and equipment. She wondered what it would be like to use some of that. She'd often thought about getting a job at a bakery over here, but the early morning hours and childcare didn't mix. She tried it once but it had ended in disaster when she had to bring a toddler with her at three in the morning. The library job was better in the long run anyway, given her work with the sisters. Baking at a bakery was something she did back in Cascadia.

"I just couldn't figure out how to do it over here."

"Everything changed that day," he mused, twisting his paper cup.

Nodding, she licked some frosting from her thumb and noticed his eyes darken. He reached out, brushed a crumb from her chin.

"Did you have any help when you...ah...got here?" he asked cautiously. You couldn't be too careful when talking about the two worlds. Some people over here refused to admit that there even *were* two worlds, a fact she found hard to believe.

She brightened. "Mariah was great. We stayed with her until I got on my feet. Found a job I liked that would support Darius and me, an apartment."

"Was there nothing for you...over there?"

She looked up at him, unsure why he was asking. "At the time, no. Not really. Things with my stepfather got so bad that I left home. My mother has never met Darius."

It was a rainy fall afternoon when she told her mother and stepfather that she was pregnant. She recalled how her stepfather had slapped her when she refused to tell him who the father was.

"Jesus, Zara. I can't imagine how hard that must have been. I'm..." A shadow passed in front of his face as he ran a hand through his hair. "I'm sorry for everything that happened. I wish I had been there for you." His voice was so strained, he could barely finish.

She reached across the table, grabbed his hand and squeezed. "Things worked out for me, though. Darius is happy, and I'm doing some good in the world by helping the sisters." She lowered her voice. "And I'm breaking gorgeous bad boys out of prison."

His mouth quirked, but he remained silent. She took that as an opportunity to ask him a little more about his time in the Institute. "Did you have friends there?"

He played with a few stray cupcake crumbs on the table then nodded. "Guys just like me with their own stories to tell."

She didn't want to think about all the other destroyed lives. "What were your days like? Did you work on the chain gang everyday?"

His face hardened, and she sensed his walls going up. She'd pushed him too far.

"Yeah," he said. His voice was so low that she strained to hear it. "But only on the days Talents weren't being used as human guinea pigs for a sick motherfucker's experimental drugs."

A FEW HOURS later when they were back at Reckless, Zara walked past the break room on the way to Rand's office and cringed. Even though the wall-mounted flat screen was on mute, she could see that the news vlogs were broadcasting stock images of cars that were the same make, model and color as hers. A witness had recently come forward with a description of a vehicle they'd seen in the backcountry area near where Vince had escaped. It felt as if a noose was tightening around her neck. First AIU and now this.

The door to Rand's office was open. He was at his desk, hunched over a handheld, and poking the screen with a stylus. He wore a short sleeve T-shirt stretched tightly over his bulky tattoo-covered biceps, and his dark hair was tousled, as if he'd been frustrated and had been running his hands through it.

She knocked lightly, and he looked up. "Hey, Zara, come on in. Have a seat." He pointed to a chair on the other side of his desk.

"Thanks." She moved a stack of automotive catalogs and sat down, then handed him the paint chip samples he'd given her earlier. "I picked one. I'm hoping it's not a premium color."

She'd taken him up on his offer to paint her car, but she didn't want to spend much.

"Already?" he asked, quirking a brow. "That was fast. I'm impressed."

In truth, she didn't give a crap what color her car was. All she cared about was that it was different from what it was now. She pointed to one of the grays. "I'm looking at this one."

"That's a standard one, all right."

"Then let's go with it."

He buzzed the paint shop and told them the color she'd chosen.

"Thanks for being able to get it in so quickly. I really appreciate it." Then she thought about the apartment, and how he'd offered Vince a job. Rand was taking a tremendous risk harboring the two of them here. "And everything else you've done to help us out."

He waved off her gratitude. "It's no problem. I'm glad to help."

Rand had lost his wife in a terrible tragedy involving the Pacifican army, so his hatred of them ran deep. She'd learned that many of the men he employed had their own grievances with the army as well.

Zara noticed a framed photograph of Rand and a young girl. "Is that your daughter?"

"Yeah, that's Caitlyn. She's nine."

"She's adorable." Zara thought about a similar photo she had of Darius and an intense longing gripped her once more. This was the longest they'd ever been apart.

As she rose to go, she saw a truck pull up in the parking lot. Perfect timing. It was probably a customer or a sales rep. But then she did a double take when the man climbing out of the vehicle had a tall, wiry-haired dog with him.

"Asher?"

Rand looked out the window. "Unless that's his body double, I'd say yes," he quipped.

How did she not know her brother was coming? What about the roadblocks? Did he have Darius with him?

She bolted out of Rand's office, excited at the prospect of seeing her son, but as she rounded the corner, she ran headlong into a muscular brick wall.

"Ack!" She flailed her arms.

Vince gripped her elbows and set her back on her feet. She'd have landed on her butt if he hadn't caught her. She looked up into his face, her heart pounding even more than it had been.

"Where are you going in such a hurry?" he asked.

"Asher just got here. He might have Darius."

Vince's mouth tightened.

"Come on." She tugged on his hand but let it slip when he didn't move fast enough.

She burst through the front door just as Asher was reaching for the handle.

"Where's Darius?" she asked, looking past him in the direction of his truck. She could see through the windshield but didn't spot anyone. "Isn't he here? Is he all right…?"

Asher chuckled. "Miss him much?" She glared at him to cut the crap. "They're fine, Z-boo. I left as soon as I heard some of the roadblocks had been lifted. Darius wasn't up yet. Figured I might be able to get you back home before he got home from school. Didn't want you driving your car."

She tried to hide her disappointment that she'd have to wait a while longer to see her son. "So you've been watching the news vlogs. I can't believe someone saw us up there."

"Maybe Rand can get rid of your car for you. Sell it. Part it out or something."

She told him about it being painted, but he shook his head. "I don't know, Zara. It's still probably safer to dump it. You'll have to change out the plates, scratch off the serial numbers. I'll talk to Rand."

The door she'd just come from slammed behind her.

Asher held out his hand. "Hey man, you must be—"

A flash of movement.

And then Vince punched Asher in the stomach, knocking him to the ground.

She gasped. "Vince, oh my God!"

Asher sprang to his feet, ready to throw a punch of his own. Conry, standing at Asher's side, growled at Vince and bared his teeth.

"Stop!" She jumped between the two men and pressed her palms to Vince's chest. His eyes were as dark as she'd ever seen them. She didn't *ever* want to be on the receiving end. "This is Asher. My brother."

"You think I don't know that?"

"Then what the fuck was that for?" Asher groused, brushing the dirt from his clothes.

"For putting Zara in danger."

"*Me?*" Asher was incredulous. "What the holy hell are you talking about?"

Vince turned to Zara, a muscle in his jaw flexing. "Has he always been such an idiot?"

Now it was Asher's turn to lunge at Vince.

"Stop!" Her feet scuffled on the gravel in her attempt to push her brother away. "Both of you. You need to calm down. You're acting like a couple of cocked-up schoolyard bullies."

Before either man could respond, a car drove around the corner of the building. A customer, potentially. They couldn't argue like this in front of ordinary Pacifican citizens, so she grabbed both men by the arm and dragged them across the parking lot to the entrance of the motocross park where no one would be able to hear them.

She let go but stayed between them. "What is going on, Vince?"

The walk hadn't cooled Vince's temper, and he glared at Asher. "You sent her in to rescue me. Alone."

"Bullshit. She was not alone. She had backup. I was there."

"Really? Where?" Vince spread his palms wide and

looked around as if he were dramatically reenacting the scene. "A couple of inept losers on the other side of the railroad tracks who couldn't even subdue a dog? Ha. I'd hardly call that backup. She could've easily—*easily*—been killed or captured. You have no fucking idea what they would've done to her, but I do."

"You're calling me inept?"

"Actually, I think I just called you a loser."

Asher flexed his fists.

Oh jeez. Not again.

Zara pointed a finger at both men. "Stop it. Both of you."

"Believe me," Asher said, not taking his eyes off of Vince. "I tried to talk her out of that hare-brained scheme of hers. And now that I've had the bloody misfortune of meeting you, I wish I'd have tried harder."

Zara's patience was wearing thin. "For your information, Vince, my brother did try to talk me out of it, but in case you hadn't noticed, I'm a big girl and can make my own decisions. I told him I was going with or without him. He had no choice but to throw together a quick plan. And *you*," she said, turning to Asher, "you think my hare-brained idea was any less ridiculous than waiting months for the Iron Guild to make a decision on whether or not to help us?"

"It was the safer choice by far." Asher crossed his arms over his chest.

Vince frowned. "The Iron Guild?"

"Yeah, we're a group of warriors who—"

"I know what the Iron Guild is," Vince said impatiently. "You asked them to help get me out? Why?"

"Because we help out our people," Asher replied.

"I'm not one of your people."

"But your mother is." Asher laughed, his tone biting. "So is Zara. And for some reason that defies all logic, she seems to really be into you."

Vince looked as though he was going to come to blows with her brother again, but instead, he spun on his heel and strode across the parking lot to the motorcycle he had borrowed from Rand.

He couldn't just leave like that.

"Vince, wait!" she called after him.

Ignoring her plea, he revved the engine and took off in a spray of gravel. Zara stood and watched as he disappeared around the end of the building.

Asher brushed the dirt from his jeans and gave Conry a pat on the head.

"Why are you into an asshole like that?" he asked. "I mean, I get that he's the father of your son, but come on."

"He's not an asshole." How could she explain to her brother that Vince was complicated and just needed some time to sort out his new life? He'd suffered all sorts of trauma while at the Institute and, more than likely, was suffering from PTSD.

Asher flicked a few of his braids behind his shoulder. "Is the dude hung like a horse or something? Is that why you're so into him?"

Now it was her turn to punch her brother. Right in the face.

*a*sher sat at the table in the break room holding an icepack to his jaw.

Oh please.

It wasn't like she'd hit him very hard. He was doing the ice-thing for the attention, and it seemed to be working, too. Melanie, the office manager, was the one who'd gotten him the ice, and a mechanic had grabbed a box of tissues in case his nose started bleeding.

After they left, he grinned at Zara as if he knew that *she* knew it was just an act.

Honestly, he hadn't changed a bit since they were kids. A fact she found both comforting and maddening.

Behind him, the flat screen was still muted. However, it was on multichannel mode now and three vlogs shared the screen.

NWX was using the headline *The Hunt for a Convict.*

SeaPac was calling it *On the Run from the Law*. And Birdie Lyons' show was using Vince's inmate photo grunged-up and stamped with the graphic, *Deadly, Dangerous and Deranged*.

Really?

How could Pacificans watch this garbage twenty-four-seven? It gave her a headache, and not just because they were talking about Vince.

She still couldn't believe he'd picked a fight with her brother. Although Vince was totally and completely off base with his accusations, and she was upset with him for storming off on his motorcycle before they'd had a chance to work things out, she was humbled he cared so much about her safety and well being. Every time the front door opened, she popped her head out of the break room, hoping it was him.

Rand came in and poured himself a cup of coffee. "So you want to sell the car instead of painting it?"

Asher must have said something to him.

"I'm just not sure it's worth the risk to keep it." She pointed to the screen. "They've been talking and speculating about that car nonstop."

"Will you be able to sell it and hide the ownership trail?" Asher asked.

Rand raised a brow. "Does a bear shit in the woods when there's no one around to see him?"

Asher laughed then turned to Zara. "I say let him have the car."

It would just be a matter of time until the news vlogs speculated that it might have been painted. They'd already been showing artists' renditions of what Vince could look like now. "Okay."

"Let me make a few calls and see what I can do," Rand said, then headed back to his office. Zara assembled a plate of cupcakes and set them in front of Asher as an unspoken peace offering.

"Thanks." He looked over all of them and started with the one that had the most sprinkles. "I'm sorry I was a dick earlier. That was uncalled for."

Yeah, it was. Looking back on it now though, it secretly made her laugh.

"Next time I'll try to have a ruler on hand, so you can measure yourselves to see who wins."

Asher grinned, holding up the half-eaten cupcake as if he were toasting her with a glass of champagne. "Might makes right."

The door out front opened again, but before she could check to see if it was Vince or not, she heard the heavy thud of boot steps coming down the hallway. He swept into the doorway as if he owned it, his muscular frame filling up the space. His face was ruddy from being windblown. A sweat mark from his helmet creased his forehead and there were mud stains on the lower part of his jeans.

She inwardly sighed. She'd take a rough-edged working man with muscles and tats who looked out for his woman, no matter the cost, over a pretty boy in suit any day of the week.

Speaking of which…

He grabbed the back of his sweatshirt and pulled it over his head, giving her a peek-a-boo view of his well-defined abs and a few of his tattoos.

"Hey," she said, as casually as she could. She didn't want to make a big deal about him storming off.

He cast her a dangerously sexy glance. Zara's heart pounded, and she found it extremely hard to stay calm when all she wanted to do was jump into his arms and kiss the hell out of him.

Vince strode over to where Asher was sitting and extended his hand. "I appreciate what you did. Sorry for the outburst." His tone was gruff, but sincere. It wasn't easy for a man like him to admit when he was wrong.

If he wasn't careful, she *was* going to jump him right here.

Asher shook his hand. "Don't worry about it. I'd have done the same thing, actually. I tend to lose my shit when Olivia's safety is involved, so I get it."

Conry growled at Vince. He, for one, *didn't* forgive that easily.

Asher patted him on the head. "It's okay, boy. We're cool." But Conry continued to glare at Vince.

Vince frowned and looked at the icepack. "What's that for? I was pissed, but I would've remembered hitting you in the face."

Asher jerked his chin in Zara's direction. "Ask her."

Zara bit her lip to keep from smiling.

Yeah, I'm a badass and don't you forget it.

"Because he bugs the ever-living crap out of me sometimes, that's why."

Asher threw his head back and laughed. "Sibling affection. Isn't it grand?"

Amusement sparkled in Vince's eyes, as if he couldn't wait to find out what the punch was all about.

"Even though I've not known Olivia for long," Zara said to Asher, "I'm pretty sure she would've approved of my actions."

"So, speaking of siblings and my sister," Vince said, walking over to the counter and opening up the cupcake container. "How is she doing? I...I really miss her."

Zara had a small private moment. She *loved* that he sought out her food.

"As well as can be expected, considering that she's shacking up with the likes of me." Asher laughed again. Guffawed, actually.

Zara snorted. The guy was his own biggest fan.

"What?" Asher asked, narrowing his gaze at her.

"Nothing." She was glad her brother was so happy... even if he was mildly irritating.

As the men talked amongst themselves, Zara noticed the screen again.

Birdie Lyons was looking as flamboyantly outlandish as she had when Zara had seen her in person at the museum. She wore another fascinator, but this one was royal blue. It was perched on the edge of her head, practically defying the laws of gravity. The woman must use all sorts of pins and spray just to keep it from sliding off.

She was broadcasting from the back seat of a moving car—from the looks of it, a limo—and speaking into a hand held camera, making the viewer feel as if they were riding along with her.

"That woman is nuts," Asher said, grabbing the remote. "But so entertaining."

The only thing entertaining about Birdie was her clothes.

Before she could stop him, he'd made Birdie's face full screen and unmuted the sound.

"...coming to you from a top secret location near New Seattle. We've just gotten a lead in the case of deranged convict, Vince Crawford, who injured three innocent men—one critically—when he escaped from the maximum security prison at the Institute just days ago. Our sources have confirmed that he had help from the outside, and we believe we know the identity of the individual who may have helped him. She—yes, my friends," Birdie said conspiratorially, pulling the camera in closer, "I said *she*. We're heading to her house now, and you're coming with to see it with your own eyes.

"So...are they a modern day Bonnie and Clyde? You tell me, folks. We've reported on several strong-arm thefts in the area. Or could they be star-crossed lovers, pining for each other but unable to be together until she released him from his shackles? Or—" Birdie held up a manicured finger "—is she a prison bunny? If you tuned in yesterday, you saw our exposé on Vincent Crawford. Women have been writing to him for years, even though it was highly unlikely he would ever be released. These women..."

Zara had heard enough. "Can you turn it off? I'm sick of hearing that bitch's lies."

She retrieved the now-empty plate of cupcakes and started to turn away, but something in the background behind Birdie caught her attention. The limo was passing a white steepled church that looked a lot like St. Michael's, the Catholic church in her town. She couldn't tell for sure, however, because Vince's prison photo was super-imposed in the corner of the screen. Birdie hadn't said what city she was in, only that she was near New Seattle.

Asher put his feet on the table and grabbed the remote. "Are you two packed? What do you need to do before we can get out of here?

"Hold on." Zara stepped closer to the screen, her heart pounding. "I want to see this for a sec."

Asher rolled his eyes. "First she hates her, now she loves her."

Zara ignored him.

In that slightly British accent of hers, Birdie was still

talking about Vince and those so-called prison bunnies, but Zara wasn't listening any more. In fact, she could hardly breathe.

Vince stepped closer and laid a hand on her wrist, his face masked in concern. "Zara?"

"Yeah, Z-boo, what's wrong?" Asher asked, frowning.

Her lungs squeezed further, and she wordlessly pointed at the screen. Vince and Asher stared at it, then turned back to Zara.

"*What?*" they said in unison.

Birdie's limo was driving past another building now. A school this time. And although she didn't see a sign in the background, Zara knew exactly what school they were passing.

"That's where Darius goes to school," she choked. "She's in my neighborhood. She's going to my house."

Oh my God, my baby.

Asher barked out orders. "Phone. I need a phone. Someone get me a goddamn phone."

Zara produced hers from her pocket, but Vince was the one who snatched it out of her hands.

For a heartbeat, he stared at the black screen. When he spoke, his voice was icy calm, like he was holding back a storm. "What's my sister's number?"

"But the army," Zara said breathlessly. "What if they're listening in?"

"Fuck the army."

With shaking hands, she reached over, pulled up

Olivia's number and put it on speaker. Olivia picked up on the first ring.

"Get the hell out of there," Asher ordered through gritted teeth. "They're—"

"I'm one step ahead of you, babe," Olivia said, her tone surprisingly light. "Saw an unmarked van parked at the end of the road this morning. Had a feeling something was up, so I kept D home today in case we needed to make a move. And we did. I was going to call...there...once I knew you'd arrived."

"So he's with you? Right now?" Zara asked, holding her breath.

"Yep. Sitting in front of me. He's got headphones on and he's playing a video game."

Relief turned her knees into rubber bands, and Vince wrapped an arm around her shoulders to steady her.

"Without telling us where you are, can you tell us *where* you are?" Asher asked.

Ah, Zara thought, in case the army *was* listening.

Olivia understood as well. "We're far from town at the place where D celebrated his seventh birthday."

Far from town? Zara was confused. They'd celebrated Darius's birthday that year at a local bowling alley. *In* town.

"Are you sure it was his seventh birthday, because—"

"Absolutely positive," Olivia said, not letting her finish. "You made cupcakes with bright blue frosting that stained the kids' fingers. Someone here got really pissed off about it."

Zara frowned. That did happen but—

"Remember?" Olivia asked.

Then it dawned on her. Olivia must've asked Darius in preparation for this conversation to throw off anyone who may be listening.

"Yes, I remember now," Zara said softly, the sound of her heartbeat pounding in her ears.

Vince squeezed her shoulder, drawing her closer. "So you know where they're at?"

She nodded.

Closing his eyes, he pressed his forehead to hers. He was just as relieved as she was that their baby was safe.

"Hang on," Asher told Olivia. "We'll be there as soon as we can."

Mr. Piccolo had been furious when he found several handprints of blue frosting on the walls leading to the arcade. He'd also claimed he found blue frosting in the finger holes of some of the bowling balls and said he should've charged her a damage deposit. She'd apologized profusely and tried to clean up the mess, but he'd shooed her away.

The call ended and both men looked pointedly at Zara.

"Well?"

Zara took a deep breath, trying not to freak out. "They're at Piccolo Pete's. It's a pizza parlor and bowling alley. And it's located *in* town. Literally only a few miles from my house."

"Are you sure about this?" Asher asked. "Olivia said they were far away."

"She lied."

———————

PICCOLO PETE'S was located at the end of a strip mall with a wooded hill behind it. Vince had driven the Harley with Zara pressed up behind him as they followed Asher in his truck. He could tell how worried she was, which stirred his protective feelings for her and Darius even more. He didn't care what the fuck he had to do to keep them safe—he'd do it.

They arrived in her hometown just after dark. Despite the other roadblocks having been lifted, the army was still checking cars and identification out on the main highway, but Zara knew of some back roads and got them there without incident.

They parked on a street above the hill, made their way on foot through the woods and were now standing next to a wall of Dumpsters behind the bowling alley.

Because Vince and presumably Zara were wanted by the authorities, they couldn't risk being seen in public, so Asher was going in to retrieve Olivia and Darius on his own. They'd considered calling her and telling her to come around back with Darius, but they couldn't take the chance with the phone again. It was Asher's belief that the new checkpoint was a result of that call being monitored.

Vince shoved his hands in his pockets and kicked at a piece of trash.

"Chill, bro," Asher said, clapping a hand on Vince's back. "I'll get them. Don't worry."

Vince couldn't remember feeling so powerless in his entire life. He clenched his fists and told himself not to punch one of the Dumpsters in front of him, even though that was exactly what he wanted to do.

"That's my son in there."

"And my woman," Asher countered. "Do you think I'm going to let anything happen to them? Not a stinking chance. I'll be in and out in a flash. Trust me."

Zara touched a cool hand to his cheek. "Darius hasn't met you yet anyway. He's not likely to go with you. At least, he'd better not."

Logically, he knew it made the most sense for Asher to go in alone, but emotionally, it pissed him the hell off. It didn't feel right to sit back and let someone else handle this. His son's welfare was his responsibility.

As soon as Asher left, Zara stepped in front of Vince, unzipped his coat, and wrapped her arms around his waist.

The tension in his neck and shoulders immediately abated. She was warm and smelled so good. He tucked her head under his chin and held onto her.

"Do you want me to tell him right away that you're his father?" she whispered. "Or do you want me to introduce you as a friend...for now?"

A damn good question. The first answer that popped into his head was, *why the hell shouldn't I be introduced as his father?*

Zara's curves were soft beneath his hands, and he pulled her tighter against him. For some reason, holding her close like this, inhaling her sweet, intoxicating scent, made it easier to think clearly.

A gamut of emotions swirled inside his head, but rather than acting on the dominant one—anger, like he so often did—he sifted through the others to find a more appropriate one.

He was going to be meeting his son for the first time, which both terrified and thrilled him. But he couldn't forget that his son would be meeting him for the first time, too. He considered the relationship he had with his own father, how much he'd loved and respected him.

"What would be best for him?" he asked.

"Hmmm." Her voice vibrated through his chest. "For now, at least until we get to somewhere safe where we can really talk, what if I just say that you're Olivia's brother and that you're someone special to me, too? Then we'll go from there. That might be enough information for him for right now, or he may want more. If he does, then I'll tell him the truth."

He tensed. "The truth?"

She must've sensed his trepidation because she started rubbing his back. "I'll tell him that we loved each other a long time ago. That we just met again and..." There was a pause and the air felt suddenly heavier with the words she was going to say. "And that I realized I never stopped loving you."

He held onto her as if she might slip through his grasp. Then, grabbing two fistfuls of her hair, he pulled her head back. Her doe-like eyes glistened as she looked up at him.

His heart ached as he looked at her. She was so beautiful, so perfect. How could a man as deeply scarred as him be the object of her affections? It just didn't make sense.

"You love me?" His voice sounded as if he'd been chewing on rocks.

"Do you doubt me?" There was no malice or hurt in her voice. It was just a simple, honest question. Which was how she'd been with him from the start. Simple and honest and pure.

"No, it's just that—" He couldn't go there. He couldn't open himself up like this.

He tried to pull away but she held onto him. And then the words made it to the surface on their own. "I love you, Zara. So fucking much that it scares the hell out of me."

Great. Did he just say that last part out loud? Couldn't he have just said the I-love-you part and left it at that?

She touched his cheek again and smiled. "What's so scary about love? Personally, I'm a fan of it."

He exhaled slowly. Where did he start and how could he explain his feelings without sounding utterly pathetic?

She laced her fingers behind his back as if she could sense his reluctance and that he might try pulling away. Ha. She knew him well.

"When you love someone as much as I love you and then you're finally together, you're afraid you're not good enough to deserve them. That you'll never be good enough and that you'll eventually do something to screw it up."

"You're not going to screw up."

"How do you know? I'm fucked up, Zara. Damaged. I'm not the innocent seventeen-year-old boy that you once loved. That boy no longer exists. How can you love the man I am now when you don't even know me?"

She splayed her small, delicate hand against his chest. "Because the man inside came to another world to find me. It doesn't matter how much time has passed or how many life experiences we have apart, my soul recognizes yours as its mate. The Fates brought *you* to *me* the first time and now they've brought *me* to *you*."

She stretched up on her toes and pulled his head down, pressing her nose to his. "You will always be the man for me, Vince Crawford."

His heart swelled as if it would burst from his chest. A kiss wouldn't erase his fears or the darkness festering in his soul, but he kissed her anyway.

Her lips were soft and willing against his as he slid his tongue inside. She tasted minty and sweet—a combination of cupcakes and peppermint gum. He wanted to devour her goodness and make it his own.

Already semi-hard from having her body pressed to his, he was fully erect now. She had to feel it, too. It was all he could do to keep from rubbing against her like a rutting fool.

He broke the kiss and tucked her against his chest again.

No matter what his personal desires were, he couldn't let that interfere with what was right for their son. This wasn't a Vince and Zara show anymore. Their decisions affected another living, breathing person who would grow up to live a life of his own. A person who should be happy and healthy. A person for whom Vince was responsible.

He'd go along with this for now, but if he discovered that being together wasn't the right thing for their son, then he would have to walk away.

*a*s soon as Darius came around the corner of the building with Asher and Olivia, Zara broke into a flat-out sprint, threw her arms around him and swung him up off his feet.

"Mom, you're squeezing me to death. Ack!"

She buried her nose in his blond hair. He smelled like little boy—sweaty with a heavy dose of pizza. "I'm hugging you like a Teddy bear. I'll never let you go."

"That's silly. I'm not a Teddy bear. I'm made of skin and bones."

She laughed. "Yes, you are. I'm just making up for all the days I missed." She put him down and covered his cheeks with kisses.

"Mom, stop kissing me so much. That's what Amber does."

"Oh. Sorry." He'd gotten into trouble for shoving a

girl at recess but had been too embarrassed to tell the playground teacher that it was because the girl had been trying to kiss him. With a hand on his back, Zara guided him to the edge of the woods. "I hear you've been having fun."

"Why is Auntie Olivia crying, Mom? And who's that man?"

Zara looked up to see Olivia wrapped in Vince's arms. He was gently rocking her, stroking her hair, telling her that he was fine and that he missed her, too.

"That's her brother, honey. She hasn't seen him in a very long time, so she's really happy."

Without letting go of Vince, Olivia reached out to Zara. "Thank you for bringing my brother back to me. To our family." Her face was streaked with tears, her eyes red.

"I had a lot of help," Zara said, looking over at Asher who was standing nearby holding a duffle bag.

She took the woman's hand, but instead of clasping it or giving it a little squeeze, Olivia pulled her and Darius into a group hug with Vince.

"Mom, what did you do?" Darius asked, whispering loudly from inside the circle as if no one else could hear him.

"I'll tell you when we get to the truck," she whispered back, just as loudly.

Vince knelt down in front of Darius and took the boy's hands in his. Zara's heart jumped to her throat as she watched Vince interact with his son for the first time.

The resemblance was uncanny. Same nose. Same forehead. Same stubborn mouth. If she were to guess, she'd say Vince's hair color had been the same as Darius's when he was that age.

"Your mom is a hero," Vince said, his voice cracking with emotion. "And very, very brave. You should be so proud of her."

"My mom is a hero?" Darius's eyes went wide and then he frowned. "Mom, is that true?"

"It depends—"

Darius didn't wait for her to finish and turned back to Vince. "What's your name and how come I don't know you?"

"Well," Vince said slowly, his gaze scouring every inch of Darius's face as if committing it to memory. "Your mom and I knew each other a long time ago. Before you were born. So that's why you don't know me."

Vince shook his hand, and Zara could tell her son wasn't sure what to make of it, like this was something grown-ups do, but when Vince told him his name, Darius grinned wide.

"Mom, did you hear that?"

"Which part?"

"The part about his name," he said, whispering loudly.

She didn't know where he was going with this. "Yes, honey, I did."

Darius cupped his hands over his mouth. "Did he know my dad?"

She nearly choked. Where had that come from?

Olivia was shaking her head and mouthing, "What the hell?"

Vince, his jaw practically on the ground, looked just as surprised as she was.

"Why do you ask?" Zara tried to sound like Darius's question was no big deal.

"Because that's my dad's name, too."

WHEN THEY GOT to where the vehicles were parked, Asher grabbed the helmet from Vince. "You go in the truck. That'll give you a chance to talk to Darius. Get to know him. It's a long drive to the Iron Haven."

They'd decided to head to the safe house that Rickert and Neyla were setting up to house Iron Guild warriors who came through the portal to fight the enemy. Then, after a good night's sleep, they'd make the trek into the mountains and cross through the portal into Cascadia. Not only were things too volatile to stay here, but Vince's mother was there. She may not have heard that he'd been found and rescued.

"You sure? It's colder than shit on that thing."

Asher laughed. "You forget. I grew up where we have no electricity or central heating. I'm hearty. My bones are used the cold. Hey, Liv." Olivia, standing by the truck, looked up as he tossed her the keys. "I lead. You follow."

"Yes, Tarzan." She gave him a salute and climbed into the driver's seat.

Vince chuckled to himself at her reply and then got serious again. "Thanks, man. I...I really appreciate everything you've done for my family." Yeah, he really owed the guy. "I can see how much my sister cares about you."

"My pleasure," Asher said. "And I've enjoyed hanging out with Darius. Awesome kid. Cracks me the hell up." Shaking his head, he smiled and swung a leg over the seat. "And my dog thinks he's the cat's meow."

Olivia did well, Vince thought, striding toward the truck. Despite his original opinion, Asher was a damn good guy. Guess he shouldn't have punched him.

Zara climbed into the back seat with Darius and the dog, while Vince sat up front in the passenger seat. Asher started the Harley and, with a gloved hand, motioned for them to follow. They hadn't even gotten onto the road yet before Darius was chattering a mile a minute, excited to tell Zara everything he'd done while she was gone. Vince turned in his seat, fascinated to listen to his son talk.

"The cafeteria had that really gross spaghetti

yesterday for lunch," Darius said. "I almost barfed when I saw it on Ben's plate."

Zara rearranged his backpack at their feet. "Oh, that wouldn't have been good. What did you do?"

He shrugged. "I ignored it. And then we had a lockdown and everyone freaked out because Amber said maybe that escaped convict was trying to get into our school."

Vince grimaced.

Zara looked up to see his reaction. He shrugged, gave her a twisted smile. What can you do? The news was all over the internet. It didn't shock him that the kids had heard about it.

Without taking her eyes off the road, Olivia reached out and gave his hand a squeeze.

"But we didn't have to climb under our desks, or anything."

"Well, *that's* good."

"I know! There are so many boogers under there. Seriously, Mom, it's disgusting."

They all laughed.

"Did you find out why you had a lockdown?" Zara asked.

Vince was struck once again by Zara's warmth and sincerity. She was truly interested in everything Darius said and she knew how to communicate with him. Vince could watch the two of them interact every day until he died and it would never grow old.

"Mrs. Gandy said someone saw a bobcat in the parking lot. Nicholas said it wouldn't try to break through the window to scratch us, so that's why we didn't need to hide under our desks."

"Nicholas was probably right."

Darius dug a pad of paper and crayons from his backpack. "What does a bobcat look like?"

"Like a large cat, I suppose. Do you know, Vince?"

Excited to be pulled into the conversation, he smiled. "The ones I've seen are about thirty pounds." He held out his hands. "And about this big. Like a really large housecat. They're tan with short tails and tufts of hair coming out of their ears."

Darius looked up from his paper, his expression serious. "You saw a bobcat in real life?"

Vince nodded. "Several times. And once, I even saw a cougar. But he was really far away."

Darius's eyes widened. "Really? Where?"

"I remember that," Olivia chimed in. "You wouldn't give me the binoculars."

"Maybe because you always hogged them," he told his sister. "Anyway, we saw the cougar in the woods way up in the mountains. We used to go camping a lot when we were kids."

Darius sifted through his crayons and picked out a tan one. "Like this color?"

"Looks about right." Vince's neck was getting a kink, but he didn't want to turn and face the front.

Darius started to draw on the paper, then he looked up and studied Vince for a moment. "So you didn't know my dad?"

Vince's throat tightened. Caught off-guard again, he tried not to look too surprised.

Zara's brows were lifted in a silent yes or no question. They'd agreed to tell Darius on the drive if the issue came up again rather than waiting for a better time. But then what was a better time? The boy was asking now and deserved an honest answer.

Heart pounding, he gave a quick nod. He was ready.

Zara brushed the hair from Darius's forehead. "You understand that you can't know everyone who shares the same name as you, right?"

"Yeah, I know. It's not really a thing, I just thought that— Never mind." Darius didn't look up from his drawing. He was coloring the same line over and over. He knew something was up.

"No, it's important," Zara said softly, "and it's something I wanted to talk to you about." She paused for what seemed like forever and took a breath. Meanwhile, Vince could hardly breathe. "Honey, Vince is— Well, he's...he's your dad."

Darius's head whipped up. He stared first at his mom to see if she was telling him the truth, then he looked at Vince, as if wanting confirmation.

"Yep, buddy, it's true. I'm...I'm your dad." His voice was deeper than normal. Probably because the lump in his throat had grown from the size of a marshmallow to that of a freaking elephant.

Darius looked confused. "How do you know?"

Oh man. Vince wasn't sure what the boy knew about the birds and the bees yet. He glanced at Zara for some help. She nodded her encouragement but remained silent. While he appreciated her confidence that he could answer this, he was still nervous as hell.

"Well, we...uh...loved each other and then there was a baby in your mom's tummy. And that baby was you."

Zara smiled at his response. Guess he was doing okay then.

But instead of asking more questions, Darius shoved his paper aside, buried his head in Zara's lap and burst out crying. The sound filled the inside of the truck and tore out Vince's heart.

He replayed his exact words, trying to figure out what he'd said that made Darius so upset. Was the boy...disappointed?

"Honey, what's wrong?" Zara bent over him, gently stroking his hair. "Can you tell me?"

Darius shook his head.

"Please, sweetie."

He mumbled something in her lap.

"I can't hear you."

He shifted. "How come he didn't love me enough to be my dad when I was little? Was I really bad?"

Vince couldn't hear Zara's response, but a hard knot lodged in his chest. His son thought he'd rejected him.

"Oh, little dude." He unbuckled his seatbelt, reached over the seat and rubbed his son's back. "You did nothing. I've always loved you." He turned to Olivia. "Can you signal to Asher to pull off at the next exit?" He needed to speak to his son face to face.

A few minutes later, they were parked in front of a roadside hamburger joint. Vince jumped out and opened the back door of the truck.

"Darius, can you take a walk with me? I need to talk to you about some things. Just me and you."

The boy's eyes were still red from crying, but he climbed over Zara's lap and took Vince's hand.

"Asher and I will grab some food," Olivia said. "Everyone okay with cheeseburgers?"

"D, do you want a peanut butter milkshake?" Zara asked. "I see they have them on the menu."

Darius nodded, but remained quiet.

They headed to a kids' play area next to the picnic tables. He sat Darius on a swing and knelt in front of him.

"Little dude, you did nothing wrong. Nothing. I promise."

Darius didn't believe him. "Then how come you weren't there when I was little?"

His heart stung as if it had just been stabbed.

"Before you were born, your mom and I lived really

far apart and we didn't get to see each other very much. But I loved her a lot and had big plans for our future. When we learned that you were in her tummy, we decided to get married right away and be a mommy and daddy together. But then…" He cleared his throat, unsure how to explain this next part. "Then some bad people came and took me away before I could get your mom. She didn't know what happened to me for a really long time. My mom and sister thought I must have died because they knew I wouldn't stay away from them on purpose."

"Why did the bad people take you away?"

Giving Darius a level look, he asked, "Do you know what a Talent is?"

"A person who knows magic?"

"Well, kind of. A Talent is someone who is born with a special ability, but sometimes you don't know that you have one. When the bad people found out I was a Talent, they took me away and tried to make me work for them. To do bad things that would've hurt people." *People like you and your mom.*

Darius's eyes widened. "You're a Talent?"

Vince nodded. "Yep."

"Nicholas says Talents are wicked and that they cast spells on other people. They're a-bottom-nations."

Abominations.

Vince bristled. There were a few religious groups who taught that Talents were repugnant and that the other world didn't really exist. A reverend with a popular vlog used to come into the prison to "heal" the sinners and drive the demons from their bodies. Given that they were there because they refused to use their talents for the army, it always struck him as odd that the army would allow the guy in.

"Well, Nicholas is wrong. I don't know any spells, and as far as I remember, pixie dust has never come out of these." He wiggled his fingers. "The only thing I can do is find portals to the other world, so I wouldn't call that very magical. Not like turning someone into a chicken or something."

Darius laughed. "That would be cool."

"Only if you weren't the chicken-guy."

Darius laughed again, pushing back against the swing. Vince stood and moved out of his way.

"What did the bad people want you to do?" Darius swung forward and back, gaining momentum each time.

"They wanted me to show them how to get to the other world. But that's where you and your mom were, so I told them no."

"But isn't that where the barbarians are from?"

Vince narrowed his eyes. "Who told you that? Nicholas?"

Darius nodded.

"Well, there are no barbarians over there. They're people. In fact, everyone I've met from there is very nice. Uncle Asher, your mom...you."

"*Me?*" Darius asked, bringing the swing to a halt.

Vince nodded. "Yes, you."

Darius clamped his hands over his mouth and talked through his fingers. "I used to live in the other world?"

"Only when you were really little, so if you don't remember anything, that's why."

Darius thought hard for a moment. "Did the bad people get mad at you when you didn't tell them?"

Vince could tell that he was starting to understand. "Yes, very mad. That's why they kept me away from you and your mom, even though I wanted to be with you more than anything in the world."

"Oh."

Vince could almost see the cogs spinning in the boy's head. This was an awful lot for him to comprehend at one time.

"More than anything?" Darius asked.

"Yep. Anything."

Then Darius's eyes sparkled with mischief. "More than…a peanut butter milkshake?"

Vince grinned. "Way more than a peanut butter milkshake."

Darius started swinging again. "How about a robot? One with laser beams in its eyes."

Vince stood behind him and pushed. "I'd take you and your mom over a robot with laser beams for eyes any day of the week."

"How about a billion times infinity?"

"That's a lot."

"That's how much my mom loves me."

"Yeah, well, *more* than a billion times infinity." It occurred to him that it was all true, not just a silly game he was playing. He did want to be a husband to Zara, a father to Darius. A whole helluva lot. Maybe once they got to Cascadia, he could begin to put his awful memories behind him. Focus on the future for once instead of trying to right the past.

Vince continued to push Darius in the swing until he saw Olivia and Asher holding up several paper sacks.

"Food's ready," he said.

Tears stung his eyes as Darius grabbed his hand on the way back to the truck. He was starting to make inroads with his son, and a huge weight lifted from his shoulders.

It was almost unbearable that Darius thought he'd been the cause for Vince not being a part of his life, when nothing could be further from the truth.

CHAPTER FOURTEEN

A thin woman covered in tattoos flitted around Dr. Uri Dobrynin, blotting makeup on his forehead, brushing lint from his suit and arranging his hair.

Good God. The attention these video people paid to their appearances boggled his mind. In all his seventy-nine years, he'd never once worn face makeup.

The woman stepped aside and turned his chair. "How's it look?"

He examined his reflection in the mirror. No shine on his forehead, his coloring was tanned and even, and his hair appeared thicker than normal.

"Not bad," he grinned. Hell, he looked ten years younger. Maybe these video people were on to something.

The woman pressed her lips tightly together. "Try not to smile so wide when you're on camera."

He was about to ask why when heels clacked in the hallway. "How're you doing, Doc?" It was Birdie Lyons' personal assistant. "She's almost ready for you."

Ready for me? Shouldn't the woman be waiting for him? After all, *he* was a guest on *her* show.

Uri was whisked into a small studio with a fake backdrop of New Seattle behind a glass desk. Birdie sat on one of two stools and wore a bright pink monstrosity on her head that matched her lips and suit. A technician was at her feet, adjusting the position of a light shining on her legs.

"How's it look?" the man yelled.

"Jesus. We're not doing a vaj shot," was the reply from somewhere behind the cameras. "A little to the left and down."

"Doctor, welcome. Please, have a seat." Birdie held out her hand but didn't lean forward. He had to stretch over the table to clasp it. "I'll do a quick introduction and then we'll get started, okay?"

"Did you get my bio? It should've been emailed to someone on your staff."

The anchorwoman flicked her hand. "Too long so we pared it down. The viewers have short attention spans. Can't give them a reason to surf to another channel, now can we?"

Somewhat irritated, the doctor sat back on the stool.

Hearing from the head of the Institute wasn't reason enough to stay tuned?

A cameraman held up his hand. Birdie sat straight and gave a plastic smile.

"Hello, everyone. I'm Birdie Lyons and this is the Lyon Report. Today, we're in the studio with Dr. Uri Dobrynin. He's the director at the prison from which convict Vincent Crawford escaped." She turned slightly in her chair. "So, Doctor, can you tell us what was going on in the prison the day this happened?"

What about the introduction? The bio that listed all his accomplishments and degrees? "Um…uh. It…was…a normal day, I guess."

"So you're saying that it's normal—" she finger-quoted and winked at the camera "—for convicts to escape from your facility on any given day?"

Uri sputtered. "Of course that's not what I'm saying." He looked around for Bradford, his personal bodyguard, but the lights were too bright.

She consulted a tablet in front of her. The back of the device, the side pointing to the camera, was covered in pink crystals. "According to my sources, quite a large number of dangerous criminals, all Talents of some degree or another, have escaped from the Institute since you started your research." She looked into the camera. "Dangerous criminals like Vincent Crawford, ladies and gents." She turned back to the doctor. "Can you tell us how something like that can happen in what is supposed to be a maximum security facility?"

The doctor quickly collected his thoughts. "While there have been some escapes, that number went way down when we started using Impedio, a drug that blocks a Talent's special ability."

"And was Vincent Crawford on this so-called Impedio?"

"Yes, he was."

Birdie nodded her head thoughtfully. "Doctor, can you tell us what Vincent Crawford's Talent is? Just what is it that makes him so valuable?"

The doctor grimaced. "I'm afraid that's classified information."

"Classified, huh?" Birdie raised an eyebrow at the camera. "Folks, my sources say Crawford's talent has something to do with portals." She turned back to the doctor. "Can you at least confirm that?"

Who the hell were her sources? Someone on his staff? If so, someone was going to pay. "No, uh, I'm afraid not."

Unfazed, Birdie smiled. She shuffled some papers on the desk in front of her; pretended to be reading them. They were blank. It was all for show. "Let's switch gears for a moment then, shall we?"

Uri was sweating under these lights. Things were progressing much faster than he had anticipated.

"A car matching the description of one seen at the

time of the escape has been traced back to a woman who lives in Roseville with her son. A little digging on our part and we learned this woman hasn't shown up for work since before Crawford's escape." She turned back to the camera. "I know what you're thinking. What about the roadblocks, Birdie? The whole region has been hamstrung and many people haven't been able to get to work. I agree. However," she held up a finger, "according to the woman's landlady, a couple had been staying at her residence to watch the woman's son. And, no, the woman wasn't on vacation. We don't believe it's a coincidence. We believe this woman helped him escape." She swiveled back toward Uri and asked pointedly, "Doctor, what exactly is the relationship between her and Crawford?"

Anger roiled inside him. Birdie Lyons was grasping at straws, inventing gossip when there was no story. He was done trying to cooperate. He'd get up and end this ludicrous interview right now, but he wasn't sure how that would come across on camera. "There are no conjugal visits at the Institute, if that's what you're asking. The prisoners are not allowed visitors of any kind."

Birdie motioned with her finger for the camera to come closer. Almost instantly, a short musical clip began to play in the background. The doctor didn't know if he was still on camera or not, so he glanced at the monitor. The screen showed a close-up of Birdie with a graphic that said *A Little Birdie Told Me*, but then it swung over and focused in on him.

He blinked, confused. What was going on? It occurred to him, too late, that he might be being railroaded.

"Doctor, a little birdie told me something very interesting."

"Uh...um..."

"We believe that this woman and Crawford used to be lovers. And that her boy," she said slowly, pausing to heighten the drama, "is Crawford's son."

Vincent had a son? That was the most absurd thing he'd ever heard. Choking on his spittle, the doctor stood from his stool so quickly that it clattered to the floor behind him. "Impossible."

A pink feather on her headpiece dipped and bobbed. "The boy and his mother have been living right under your nose. This. Whole. Time."

Now it was his turn to look smug. This woman was all about fluff and ratings. Her quote unquote facts were nothing more than figments dreamed up by a staff who should be writing fiction, not news stories. "The man has been locked up for years. He's had no visitors. Hell, even his family didn't know where he was."

Birdie rolled her eyes at the camera, winked, then turned back to the doctor. "So you're saying it's impossible to father a child when you're—" She counted on her fingers for the audience's benefit, "—eighteen years old?"

"That's not what I'm— No, we would've known…" Where the hell was Bradford? He was supposed to be nearby.

"A simple check into the woman's background shows nothing beyond eight years ago. Nothing. Her son is ten. This confused us at first." Then her perplexed frown transformed into a slow, confident smile. "But then we figured it out. Ladies and gents, we believe the woman is…" she paused again, "…from Cascadia." Dramatic music, like an audio exclamation mark, surged throughout the studio and ended on a single violin note that held as Birdie finished her point. "And that this boy was conceived over there after Crawford visited through a portal."

The music faded away, and Uri's head began to pound. What the hell was she talking about? This couldn't be possible. But even as he thought that, images of Vincent's drawings flashed in his head. That girl was over here now? How could he have missed that? And she…they had a son? He'd pumped Vincent so full of truth serum, and he'd revealed lots of secrets. Surely he'd have admitted he had a son and that the woman he loved was over here.

Unless…

Vincent hadn't known.

Birdie was still talking. "I'd like to know, as would

my viewers, what's to prevent them from running through a portal and escaping back to Cascadia?"

Now it was the doctor's turn to laugh. "They can run, but they can't hide." He cringed at how unoriginal that sounded, but it was true. He wanted her goddamn audience to know he meant business.

He started to say more but stopped himself. Birdie and her viewers didn't need to know that he had people over there right now setting up a sleeper-cell, thanks to the information Vincent had given him while under the influence of the truth serum.

The problem with the army was that they only knew how to use force and might to achieve their goals, when perhaps the best way was to infiltrate the enemy and get them to trust you first.

CHAPTER FIFTEEN

The Iron Haven was nestled in a remote wilderness area surrounded by a swirling layer of fog so thick it could have been a low-lying cloud. Even though it was late, a couple was waiting for them on the front steps. The man wore a kilt, his arm draped casually around the woman's shoulders.

"That's Rickert and Neyla," Olivia whispered so as not to wake Darius.

Zara stood at the door as Vince gently lifted their sleeping son from the back seat of the truck and carried him inside. They followed Neyla down a hallway and into a small bedroom. She pulled back the comforter on one of the beds and removed several hot water bottles scattered on the sheet.

"We don't have central heating," she whispered, "so it gets pretty cold back here."

"Mama?" Darius mumbled as Vince laid him down.

"Right here, baby." Zara bent and kissed him on the forehead. "You go back to sleep now, okay?"

He grabbed her arm to keep her from leaving. "Where are you going?"

"I'll just be in the next room, talking to the grown-ups."

"But I don't want to be by myself."

"You're not, buddy, I'll—"

"I'll stay with him, Zara," Vince said from behind her. "If that's okay with you, little dude?"

Zara had no idea what the two of them had talked about on the swing set, but evidently it had been impactful.

"Clear over there?" Darius looked at the other twin bed only a few feet away as if it were a mile.

"Do you want me to lie here with you till you fall asleep?"

Darius frowned. "I want you to stay here all night."

"Tell you what. I'll stay till you fall asleep, then I'll go talk to the grown-ups for a little bit, then I'll come back. But you have to promise me something."

"What?"

"It's really important."

"Okay, okay," Darius said impatiently.

"No snoring."

Darius clamped a hand over his mouth and laughed. "I don't snore."

Vince flashed a conspiratorial smile. "Well, when your aunt Olivia was your age, she snored really loud. I used to tease her that she sounded like a pig."

Darius snickered.

"Shhh. Do *not* tell her I told you that. She'll kill me."

Zara saw what Vince was doing. He was getting Darius to focus on something funny instead of worrying about the negative. Very clever.

Darius settled into the pillow and seemed satisfied with that plan.

Vince looked at Zara. "Well, I guess that's that. I'll see you in a bit." He kicked off his shoes, tossed his coat on a chair, and climbed onto the bed. "Oh man, it's so narrow."

Darius rolled his eyes. "You're too big to lie on your back. You need to lie on your side. Here, like this." Darius grabbed Vince's shoulder, pulling and pushing him until he had him situated just so.

"See?" Darius patted the sheet. "Now there's room for me right here." He scooted closer, grabbed Vince's muscular arm and snuggled underneath it.

Vince had a contented smile on his face, like there was nowhere else he'd rather be than right here. "You seem like an old pro, like you've done this a few times."

"Yeah, me and my mom like to snuggle, so I'm pretty good at it."

The last thing Zara heard before she slipped out the

door was fake snoring and pig snorting sounds—*oh great* —then Darius asked Vince to tell him a story.

WHEN VINCE ENTERED the great room the next morning, the smell of fresh-brewed coffee hit him like two-by-four. How long had he slept anyway? He looked around. Late, apparently.

Zara and Neyla stood on opposite sides of the massive dining table, smoothing out a large piece of fabric. Asher and Olivia were lying on a couch near the fire.

Zara looked up and her face brightened. "You're awake. Did you sleep well?"

"Apparently, I did," he said, yawning.

"Morning," Neyla said over her shoulder.

"Good morning, sunshine," Olivia called from across the room.

Asher lifted a hand. "Yo."

Zara came around the table and hugged him. He pulled her close with one hand and slipped the other hand down to caress her bottom, loving how her soft curves felt against him. She moved subtly against his growing erection.

"Good God, woman," he whispered in her ear and she laughed softly.

And then he thought about their son. No, he and Zara would have to wait.

"I didn't expect to fall asleep like that," he said. "Figured I'd be there five, ten minutes tops after I told Darius a few stories. He liked the one about slaying dragons the best, by the way."

"Sounds like the perfect story." Her beautiful face was turned up to him, her gray eyes twinkling.

Even though it had been less than a day, her gentle encouragement that he was on the right track as a father meant a lot to him. Rather than hovering around, telling him what he should be saying or doing, she trusted that he'd figure it out his own way, and it meant the world to him.

"Speaking of...where is our son?"

"You just missed him. It snowed last night, so he went outside with Rickert. You hungry? We made a huge breakfast scramble."

So *everyone* was up? Having not seen Rickert yet, he'd figured the guy was still sleeping. His stomach growled. He'd shovel something in quickly then go outside with Darius.

Zara started into the kitchen, but he grabbed her wrist to stop her. "I can get it. Looks like you're busy."

She looked up at him from beneath her dark lashes, smiling softly. "Are you sure...?"

He loved how she wanted to take care of his physical needs. "I've got it, babe, but thanks." He bent down and gave her a quick, hard kiss on the lips, which left him aching for more, and then he reluctantly stepped away.

Soon, he was leaning against the counter overlooking the great room, eating a huge mound of eggs and potatoes with more than a few squirts of green Tabasco. The best condiment ever. God, he'd missed this stuff.

The two women were doing some sort of project involving a large piece of fabric. If he hadn't already known that Neyla used to be a badass lieutenant in the army, he never would've believed it. She was what he'd call a girly-girl—into clothes, makeup and fashion. She'd once been a costume designer with her own business, but when her latent Talent had manifested, she was forced to give that up and join the army. She'd since gone back to what she'd done before.

Little chance of that happening for him. You couldn't exactly go to a prestigious art school when you're wanted by the authorities. He was a different person now anyway.

He thanked Neyla for her part in getting him out of prison, but she tried to brush it off as no big deal. "All I did was make a few calls."

"I'd still be there if you hadn't obtained the intel you did. Once you step foot inside those walls, you pretty much disappear off the face of the earth."

She sighed heavily. "Yeah, there are all sorts of rumors floating around in the Talent ranks about what goes on there. You did something that all of us deep down wished we were brave enough to do—you stood up to the army. I'm just glad I could help."

"If only I could figure out a way to get the rest of them out, I would."

Zara lifted her head, her brows pulled tightly together. "You'd actually consider going back there?"

"I wouldn't want to go back if my life depended on it, but they don't deserve to be there any more than I did."

He carried his plate to the window, expecting to see Darius playing in the snow. A fresh layer of white powder covered the ground and the vehicles, but all he saw were two sets of tracks leading from the porch into the woods. "Do you know where Darius and Rickert went?"

Neyla flashed him a sheepish smile and rubbed her slightly rounded belly. "To indulge one of my cravings. But don't worry. They didn't go far."

Sure enough, he had just finished washing and drying his plate when the main door opened, and Darius burst inside, bringing with him a cold gust of air. Rickert was right on his heels.

"Dad, grab some glasses. Hurry."

Zara cleared her throat. "I didn't hear *please*."

"Oh, sorry," Darius said, wiping his nose with the back of his hand. "Grab some glasses, please."

It took Vince a moment to collect himself. His son had called him *dad* for the first time. His chest welled with pride, and when he looked over at Zara to gauge her reaction, he saw a faint sheen of tears glistening in her beautiful eyes.

Oblivious to what was going on, Rickert placed a carton of chocolate milk on the counter.

"Did you go to the store?" Vince asked, confused. He thought the nearest town was several hours away.

"I put this out in the snow when I got up." The other man filled several glasses, handing one to Neyla and one to Darius. "*Someone* had a craving for a milkshake, but slushy chocolate milk was the best I could do."

Darius licked his chocolate milk mustache but missed the corners. "Yum."

"It's perfect," Neyla said. "Thank you, boys."

She turned back to her project, but Rickert came up behind her and wrapped his arms protectively around her waist. "Why don't you sit down? You don't need to work on that now, do you?"

"I want to finish this before we leave. Who knows when I'll be back?" she said, patting her slightly rounded belly.

"How many other Havens are there?" Vince asked curiously.

"This is the first," Rickert replied. "But we'd like to set up a few others, with one on the peninsula being the next on the list."

"You're not afraid of Pacifican soldiers finding them?" Vince asked.

"Did you happen to notice the fog when you came in?"

Vince nodded. It was so thick that they almost lost sight of the Harley's taillight just a few feet in front of them.

"It's an illusion created by placing Esmerelda glass strategically around the perimeter of the property," Rickert explained. "Unless you have a shard from one of the crystals and know exactly where to go, you'd never find the place." The other man pulled a pendant from a chain around his neck. "All the warriors wear them now."

"The *Taghta* sisterhood uses a similar method to keep their abbeys hidden," Zara chimed in. "But I didn't realize Esmerelda glass would survive a portal crossing."

Rickert nodded. "They've got flecks of iron, so it's one of the few items that does. But you do deal with more portal sickness when you cross."

"A necessary side effect." Asher strode into the kitchen, ruffling Darius's hair as he passed, and leaned against the counter. "I'd rather deal with that and have a place of our own than live like nomads when we're over here. So you'll be working on finding a location for the peninsula's haven after the Warrior Games?"

A shadow crossed Rickert's face "Aye. We need one. The Pacifican army is getting too close to one of the portals there, so we can't risk pulling our men. So far we've been successful, but every time we get them to retreat, they just regroup and come back. They know they're getting close. Our saving grace is that if they do get through, it's located in a very remote corner of Cascadia, and we've got people keeping watch on the other side."

"Warrior Games?" Vince asked.

Rickert explained that the Iron Guild holds a tournament where young men compete in various speed, endurance and skills competitions. The best are invited to become warriors.

"Besides, it's a huge party," Asher said, grinning. "No one wants to miss it if they don't have to."

CHAPTER SIXTEEN

he trail from the Haven into the mountains was rugged, not much more than a game trail with slight dips and indentations in the underbrush. However, Vince could've found their destination with his eyes closed.

They hadn't been walking for long when he became aware of a low thrumming just under his skin, and although it had been ages ago, he knew exactly what it was. The portal called to him like a radio beacon and he was the receiver, which was how he'd found the Granite Falls portal that had led him to Zara.

He rubbed the goosebumps on his arm. Yeah, the Impedio must be completely out of his system now.

He'd been fly-fishing with friends one summer the first time he'd felt the hum of a portal. Hobs and Jamie were on one side of mountain stream, and he had just crossed to the other side to get a better angle at the pool behind a downed tree. His fish intuition was usually pretty accurate; he knew there were rainbow trout in those depths.

His first cast had gone a little too far to the right—it was liable to get caught in the snag as it drifted downstream—but his second cast was perfect, placing the hand-tied fly atop the water in the center of the pool. Hobs had given him a silent thumb's up, not wanting to make any noise. As he waited for the telltale shimmering shape of a fish to rise from the depths and take a bite, he'd heard a faint hum, a far-off, even sound like the buzzing of an insect. Batting a hand instinctively around his face, he'd glanced around looking for angry bees. He'd stepped on a hornets' nest once, so he was always wary of buzzing noises.

"Do you guys hear that?" he'd called.

Hobs had glared at him silently. It was Jamie who spoke, holding a hand up to his mouth. "I don't hear anything."

He'd shrugged it off and made a few more casts, but the moment he went still, he heard it again. Reeling in his line, he'd set the pole down, climbed up the low river bank behind him and scanned the sky through the trees. "Are you sure you guys can't hear that? It sounds like a helicopter."

"What would a helicopter be doing clear out here?" Hobs had asked, his face contorted with impatience. He took his fishing very seriously and Vince was breaking the quiet rule.

"I don't know. Rescuing a stranded hiker or something?"

"Well, I don't hear anything," Hobs had said after a moment.

"Me either," Jamie chimed in.

Fine. Vince didn't push it, even though the humming persisted. They ended up catching and releasing several nice rainbows before heading back to Jamie's car parked at the trailhead. As he'd lain in bed that night, he couldn't get the memory of that sound out of his head, so he made plans to go back later on his own.

If only he hadn't told anyone after he'd found the portal. Hell, he didn't even know what a Talent was back then. He should've known something was wrong when Hobs started asking him all sorts of questions about the portal a few years later. By that time, he'd met Zara, so he'd downplayed his discovery, saying he didn't really remember. How was he supposed to know that Hobs' father was an army official in charge of rounding up latent Talents?

Vince was so lost in thought that he didn't notice that Darius was getting tired. Asher had, however, and hoisted the boy onto his shoulders, then pretended not to notice he was heading straight toward a low-hanging branch.

Darius clung to him. "Watch out!"

Asher ducked at the last minute, and Darius shrieked with laughter.

Vince felt a tinge of jealousy. Asher was a fun, carefree guy, unencumbered by a dark past that consumed him. A much better father figure than a man whose only goal for the past ten years had been revenge.

After side-stepping a thick patch of blackberries, the tiny hairs on his arms prickled. They were getting close. A large stump nursing two cedar saplings lay straight ahead and behind that, the terrain became rockier, angling sharply upward, the mountain simply rising out of the ground.

Rickert pointed. "It's up there."

Asher set Darius down and the boy ran the rest of the way. Glancing over at Zara, Vince noticed the tiny lines of tension around her mouth. "Nervous?"

She nodded. "A little. Haven't been back in years. Once Darius goes through, we'll be staying there. Our lives over here are gone."

Guilt gnawed at him as he reached out and rubbed her shoulders.

If a teenager couldn't be trusted to keep his mouth shut about a portal, a little boy certainly couldn't. Vince couldn't forget the serious ramifications his presence had on Zara and Darius's lives. Had they parted ways once they got to Reckless, Zara could've continued on with her life as it had been. She'd be at the library and doing the occasional job for Mariah, and Darius would still be in school. Sure, she may have faced some routine questions from the authorities because of the car, but she could've come up with a plausible story. Who would ever think that a single mother working at a library would be involved in the high-profile escape of a prisoner anyway?

When they got to the base of the cliff, Asher lifted an excited Darius up the rocks.

"I see it! A cave."

Zara turned to Vince. "Ever since he was little, he's been fascinated by them. His favorite books from the library were ones about caves and spelunking."

Vince grinned. He'd been fascinated by caves as a boy, too.

Once they climbed up the rocks, Olivia pulled a flashlight from her backpack and handed it to Darius. "Can you light the way for us?"

"Yes!" Darius snatched it from her and ran to his mom. "I can't believe we're going into another world. I'm so excited. It feels like someone's tickling my arms and legs with feathers."

Her smile looked forced. "I know how you feel, buddy. I'm excited, too."

Darius stood in the mouth of the cave and snapped on the light. "Do you think there will be bats inside? Wow, look. Stalagmites."

The temperature inside the tunnel had to be twenty degrees colder than outside. And damp. Zara managed to zip up Darius's coat before he charged ahead. After several twists and turns, a rock wall loomed ahead of them. They'd come to the end. Vince's heartbeat cranked up a notch.

They all gathered in the narrow alcove and Asher explained to Darius what was going to happen. "See that indentation in the wall? That's what I was telling you about."

Darius shined the light over the surface. "It looks like normal rock."

"I know, but it's not."

It was decided that Rickert and Neyla would go through first. Several small storage lockers were stacked against the wall. Rickert opened one and reached for the belt of his leather kilt.

"What's he doing, Mom?" Darius whispered. "It looks like he's taking off his clothes."

"He is, honey. When you go through a portal, whatever you're wearing disintegrates, so you have to take it off or...well, it'll be gone anyway. Besides, it gives them something to put on when they come back through."

Following Asher and Olivia's lead, Vince, Zara and Darius turned their backs to give Rickert and Neyla some privacy.

"See you on the other side," Neyla called from behind.

"We'll be waiting for you," Rickert said.

A rumbling noise came from deep inside the rock. When they turned around, Neyla and Rickert were gone.

Darius tugged on Zara's sleeve. She bent down and he whispered something in her ear, which made her smile. "Boy, you really *are* excited."

Now it was Vince, Zara and Darius's turn. Vince sat on top of one of the lockers and took off his boots.

"Does it hurt, Mom?"

"I've only been through a portal once—with you a long time ago. It felt strange, but, no, it didn't hurt."

Darius's eyes widened. "I went through a portal?"

"Yep. But you were really little, so you probably don't remember."

Zara stood behind Darius and removed the rest of her clothes. As Vince folded them and placed them into a storage locker, she put her hands over Darius's eyes.

"What are you doing?" he asked.

"You don't need to see your mom naked," she informed him.

"We're ready," Vince called to Olivia and Asher.

"Okay," Olivia replied from around the corner. "We'll be right behind you."

The three of them stepped into the tiny alcove. "See you in Cascadia."

With a nod of his head, they touched the wall in unison. Instantly, a frisson of energy ran over Vince's skin, and the ground beneath his feet fell away. He was struck with the simultaneous yet contradictory sensations of flying through the air at dizzying speeds yet being perfectly still.

When he opened his eyes a moment later, they were in Cascadia, all right.

A large man stood over them, holding a deadly broadsword.

ALTHOUGH IT HAD BEEN eight years since Zara had been in Cascadia, it all came back to her in a flash. The damp, earthy smell that settled over her skin and seeped into her nostrils. The sound of horses nearby snorting and stamping their hooves.

And, yes, the pounding in her head. She didn't dare open her eyes yet. Not 'til the spinning subsided.

"Toryn, they're with me." It was Rickert's voice.

"Yes, sir."

She heard a scrape of metal on metal and the rustle of fabric.

Darius tugged on her hands. "Mom, we're here."

"Yes, honey," she managed to say through the fog.

A cloth was thrust into her hands, but she wasn't sure what to do with it.

"Zara? You okay?" The concern in Vince's gruff tone was palpable. He put her arms into some sort of garment and slid it over her head.

"I'm...I'm a little dizzy is all."

"She's got a touch of the Iron sickness." Rickert's voice again. "Everyone gets it to one extent or another when they cross through, some worse than others."

Hands on her elbows, Vince gently guided her down two steps and had her sit on a cold stone bench. Only then did she crack open her eyes, careful not to let in too much light.

They were in a small stone antechamber not much larger than the apartment at Reckless. Above where she sat was the portal they'd just come through. Unlike the Pacifica side, there was no doubt what this was. The indentation was flanked by two bare-chested men in kilts brandishing large broadswords at their hips. Iron Guild warriors. They were guarding the Cascadia side of all known portals now. No one came in or out without their knowledge. A rustic wooden table was topped with dozens of candles that cast a warm, flickering glow on the walls. The whole place was almost alter-like.

Sunlight streamed through a low doorway to her left. It appeared to be the only way in or out. Darius would be able to walk through without stooping, but a tall man would have to go on his hands and knees.

Neyla, dressed in a simple blue shift, was helping Darius roll up a pair of drawstring pants that were much too big for him. "Once we get back to the castle, I'll get you some clothes that will fit better," she promised.

Vince was lacing a pair of leather breeches. She couldn't help noticing how well they fit.

A broad-chested man stood next to him. Like the guards, he, too, was wearing a leather kilt and carried an enormous sword, but rather than being bare chested, he wore a loosely tied white tunic. He held out a pair of leather moccasins.

"Here," he said gruffly, shoving them at Vince. "Is Asher coming behind ye?"

Vince took them, knelt before her, and slipped them on her feet in Prince Charming fashion. "Yes, with Olivia."

"And Conry. We can't forget him. He's there, too." Darius jumped from one foot to the other, hardly able to stay still. This whole experience was so exhilarating for him.

"Then ye'd better move on. This wee place will not hold all of ye."

The instant the words were out of the man's mouth, the air in the room crackled with electricity. Vince grabbed Zara's arm and propelled her toward the doorway where Rickert and Neyla were standing with Darius.

"I want to watch them come through, Mom," he said. "Can I?"

The man in the white tunic started to protest, but Rickert interrupted him. "Fine with me, Toryn." Then he followed Neyla out of the low doorway.

A loud snap echoed against the walls and then...

"Toryn, man, you waited." Asher's voice boomed behind her. "Did you miss me?"

"Miss ye?" Toryn snorted. "Like a toothache."

With a giggle, Darius pulled Zara down to his level. The sudden movement made her head pound even more. "Mom," he whispered loudly. "He's naked. I can see his peen."

Trying not to laugh, she patted the top of his head. "Yes, I'm sure you can. But don't stare. It's not polite." She'd have to remember to tell him that he was likely to see more than that over here. The people of Cascadia were much more open about their bodies and their sexuality than they were in Pacifica.

Conry bounded over to them and licked Darius's face. "Hey, boy!"

A few minutes later, she was outside, where bright sunlight scraped at her eyeballs.

"Jesus, Zara." Vince cradled her head against his chest, shielding her face from the light and stroking her hair. "You look sick."

"How did you go back and forth so much the summer we met?" she asked weakly. "This is brutal."

"Doesn't seem to affect me."

A small pouch was thrust into her hands.

"Have some dried *ogappa*," Neyla said to her. "It'll help settle your stomach and calm your equilibrium."

Ogappa? She'd forgotten all about the fruit. They

didn't have it over in Pacifica. Fishing out a small piece, she popped it in her mouth and chewed. The mango-like morsel was sweet and perfectly dried, with just the right amount of chewiness. She ate another piece. She'd forgotten how much she loved *ogappa*.

"Mmmm," Darius said. Evidently, he liked it too.

"Everyone okay?" It was Olivia's voice.

"Zara's got a touch of the Iron sickness." Vince's voice rumbled from his chest. He sounded worried.

The air stirred in front of her as cool, healing hands cupped her forehead and temples. Almost immediately the pounding in her head subsided. Zara opened her eyes to see Olivia standing in front of her.

"Better?" The woman's mismatched eyes were warm and caring.

She blinked a few times, moved her head around. "You...you healed me?"

"Just put you back on the right track, rather than have it run its course."

Zara looked around for the first time, testing out her head. An expression of wonder was plastered across Darius's face. He looked like a kid at a theme park. "I feel a lot better. Thank you."

She glanced at Vince and saw the tense set of his shoulders relax as he released a deep breath.

Olivia smiled. "Glad I could help."

A cart pulled by two grey horses stood in front of them. The broad-shouldered man named Toryn helped them in, while Rickert swung a leg up and over the back of a majestic black stallion.

Darius tugged at her arm, peppering her with a million questions as the cart jolted forward. She did her best to answer them.

"You're right. There are no cars over here."

"Yes, we're going to an actual castle."

"I'm sure you can learn to ride a horse."

The journey to Crestenfahl took several days. Because the town would soon be hosting the Warrior Games, the cart path was crowded with spectators, vendors, and entertainers. There were young men as well, traveling in groups or alone. They were going to be competing in the hopes of being asked to join the Guild, much like her brother had many years ago.

Having several Iron Guild warriors in their group did have its perks, however. Heads turned, people waved, and at every inn, they were given the best accommodations.

Vince hadn't said much since leaving the portal. Deep in thought, he stared off into the distance as the cart swayed, a slight frown on his face. At their first stop, he pulled Rickert aside and the two carried on a hushed conversation. The next morning, she was surprised when the stable hand saddled up a dark, big-boned gelding and gave Vince a leg up. As far as she knew, he wasn't an experienced horseman. But he took to it quickly, sitting tall in the saddle, his hands soft on the reins, legs relaxed. Asher had acquired a horse, too, and from then on out, the three of them rode together, while the women and Darius rode in the cart.

"So is this a hen house now with one little rooster?" Olivia stretched out her legs and nudged Darius with her toe.

"Seems like it," Zara said in a distracted voice.

"A rooster?" Darius asked.

She smiled despite herself. "Roosters are boys and hens are girls."

"Any idea what's going on with those two?" Olivia asked.

"Afraid not. I was hoping you did. Vince hasn't said a word..." He'd said little last night, in fact, even when she'd asked. They'd shared a large featherbed with Darius—who filled the chasm of quiet between them. "Rickert hasn't said anything to you?" she asked Neyla.

The woman shook her head, making her high blond ponytail swing across her shoulders. "I can tell he's worried about something." She rubbed her belly. "And for once, it's not the baby."

CHAPTER SEVENTEEN

*L*ocated on the top of a low rise and surrounded by rolling fields, the walled city of Crestenfahl was bustling with activity. Vendors were setting up both inside and outside the gates, selling everything from textiles to *ogappa* cider. There were jugglers, musicians and fortunetellers. Travelers without accommodations inside the castle walls were erecting colorful tents in the fields. To say that excitement and anticipation hung in the air was an understatement.

Darius sprang to his feet, feeling it too. "I didn't know there was going to be a carnival!"

"I didn't know either." She'd been to the Games once when her father had taken their family, but that was so long ago now that the details had all but faded from her memory.

Zara turned to check out Vince's reaction to all this activity. He rode alongside the cart, staring intently at the open gates. She followed his gaze, trying to figure out what had captured his attention. A silver-haired woman stood apart from the crowd, hand shading her eyes from the setting sun and looking in this direction.

Vince mumbled something and urged the chestnut forward. The horse dropped his head a notch and eased into a big, rolling canter. Zara marveled once again at how comfortable Vince seemed on horseback. At the bottom of the hill, there were too many people to navigate around, so he reined in the animal, jumped off and ran the rest of the way on foot.

Tears stung the backs of her eyes as she watched the woman run toward Vince at a much slower pace. When he got to her, he fell to his knees and wrapped his arms around her waist, like a little boy would do. The older woman tilted his face up, stared at him for a moment, and then showered him with kisses.

Darius jumped from the cart as soon as it stopped. "Mom, who is that lady?"

The answer caught in her throat as she followed him down. "That's your grandma, honey. Your dad's mom."

"It looks like she's crying."

"That's because she hasn't seen him for a very long time." She couldn't imagine what the woman had gone through, being separated from her son for so long and thinking him dead.

She was trying to decide whether to hang back to give Vince and his mother a chance to share this private moment alone, but then Olivia grabbed her hand, tugging her and Darius up the hill.

"Can you believe it, Mom?" Olivia said, laughing through her own tears as she hugged her.

"It's a miracle indeed." The woman didn't shift her gaze from Vince's face. She was soaking in every detail.

Vince swiped at his eyes and rose. "Mom, this is…" Voice cracking with emotion, he cleared his throat to cover it up.

Without waiting for him to recover, Zara smiled and extended her hand. "Mrs. Crawford, I'm Zara."

The woman's grasp was warm and strong. "So you're the one who saved my son's life." Before Zara could reply, Vince's mom pulled her into a fierce embrace that nearly knocked the breath out of her. She smelled like sugar and rosemary. "And none of this *Mrs.* business. I'm Mom or Alexandra."

"And this," Vince said, his hands on Darius's shoulders as he walked him forward, "is my son."

Darius looked uncomfortable but he went along with it.

Alexandra's face went from confusion to amazement to pure joy as the weight of Vince's words sunk in. "Your son? But…but… This…this is my grandbaby?"

Vince nodded, pride reflected in his eyes. "His name is—" he paused for effect "—Darius Vincent."

Up until now, the woman's eyes had been dry. Not any longer. Tears streamed down both cheeks as she pulled Darius close and kissed the top of his head. The boy managed to flash Zara a lopsided smile even though he was pressed against his grandmother's bosom, an awkward enough position to be in when you actually knew the person.

Alexandra kissed the back of Zara's hand, a gesture she found so charming. "You named him after Vince, who was named after his father. Thank you." Her voice caught. "You don't know how much that means to me."

Zara had a pretty good idea, though.

As they walked through the gates of Crestenfahl, Zara couldn't help thinking about her own mother. She wished that—

No, don't go there.

She'd learned a long time ago that you couldn't live someone else's life for them. You could only live your own. This...this right here would have to be enough.

———

THE MAIN DOOR of the castle creaked loudly as it opened. Once they were inside, it took a moment for Vince's eyes to adjust to the dim lighting.

They were in a great hall with a wood-beamed ceiling that soared above them and ornate tapestries lined the stone walls. Sounds of laughter and merriment came from a long table at the far end of the room. Vince turned to see an older couple approaching—a man dressed in breeches and a fine waistcoat and a woman in a silver gown.

"Welcome to Castle Crestenfahl." The man spread his hands wide. "We've been expecting you."

Rickert introduced them as Lord and Lady D'Angelus, his uncle and aunt. A little boy ran up to Rickert and the man hoisted him up.

A young woman joined them and introduced herself as Petra, their daughter.

"And how was your journey?" Lady D'Angelus asked.

"Very long," Zara replied. "But we're glad to finally be here. Thank you for your hospitality."

"It is our pleasure."

A young girl peeked her head around Petra's skirts. "There used to be a portal that was closer, but it had to be destroyed."

Rickert's jaw visibly tightened. As punishment for bringing Neyla through—a Pacifican soldier—and lying about it, he'd had to destroy the portal with a pickaxe.

"Shh," Petra said, flashing Rickert an apologetic smile. "We don't need to talk about that now."

"Come," Lord D'Angelus said. "You're just in time for evening meal."

They followed him into a great room where a huge table was set with piles of food. An uncomfortable hush fell over the twenty or so people who were seated around it, and Vince wondered if he was the cause. Neyla had told him that Cascadians, as a whole, could be very wary of strangers. Especially those from Pacifica.

Benches scraped on the stone floor as room was made around the table for them. While Zara served Darius, Vince helped himself to several roasted pieces of meat from the heaping platter in front of him. Charred corn on the cob slathered with butter. Thinly sliced vegetables that resembled green tomatoes. Thick chunks of crusty bread. Only a wooden spoon sat next to his plate. No fork or knife. He glanced around to see how people were eating. They used their spoons, their bread and their fingers. And a few were using knives that he suspected had been tucked into their belts.

When in Rome...

He grabbed a drumstick in one hand and took a bite. Tender and moist, the meat fell off the bone and melted in his mouth. He took a bigger bite. Holy fuck the sauce was good. Dark brown, rich and slightly earthy, like it was made with mushrooms. He wasted no time grabbing his bread and sopping up more.

Lord D'Angelus, seated at the head of the table, stood and tapped a knife on his tankard.

Utensils, plates and mugs clattered as everyone looked up from their plates in expectation.

"Praise the Fates," he said, lifting his drink, his voice booming through the Great Hall. "Thank you for this bountiful meal."

Everyone lifted their drinks. Vince scrambled to grab his. "Praise be the Fates," people answered in unison.

"We're here to celebrate not only the upcoming Games, but to give thanks to a great warrior in our midst."

A murmur reverberated across the table and people stirred in their seats. There were several Iron Guild warriors present that Vince hadn't met yet. He fidgeted, feeling uncomfortable and out of place.

Lord D'Angelus glanced over the crowd of people, a proud, regal expression on his face. "Vince Crawford, brother to the Healer Olivia and son to the lovely Alexandra, was imprisoned by the Pacifican army for ten years. His crime? He refused to divulge the location of a hidden portal that led straight to our world. There is no doubt in my mind that his courageous refusal to cooperate saved countless Cascadian lives. He is an outsider, you say, but that is pure hogwash. Vince has Cascadian blood flowing through his veins for his mother was but an infant when Pacificans raided a village and took her from her family."

Vince glanced over at Asher. The man was grinning ear to ear. "Did you tell him all that?"

"I wasn't the only one."

Darius sat between him, his eyes wide.

People pounded their utensils on the table and someone whistled.

Almost immediately, the tone in the room changed.

He went from zero to hero in ten seconds flat. People smiled at him. Someone clapped him on the back. With a hand on the back of his chair, a serving girl leaned forward to pour a dark red wine into his tankard. Her breasts, bursting over the top of her bodice, were just inches from his face.

"Uh, thanks," he muttered.

Her cheeks reddened, then she ducked her head and turned away.

He took another bite of his food when a young woman sitting across from him asked whether he wanted some stew. If he remembered correctly from the introductions earlier, she was one of Lord D'Angelus's daughters.

Before he could answer, Zara spoke up. "I've got it." She reached across the table, snatched the serving terrine from the surprised young woman and dished the thick stew onto his trencher.

His lips quirked at her uncharacteristic display of temper.

Mmmm. Meat. Potatoes. Carrots.

After his second tankard of wine, he started to relax. At some point during the meal, a minstrel had begun playing. The music was just background noise among the ruckus sounds at the table. Plate after plate of sweets were brought out and set before him. And each time, Zara brushed his hand away as he went to reach for them.

"I'll get it," she'd say, choosing a morsel and setting it on his plate.

Heads close together, Lord D'Angelus's daughter and the serving girl seemed to be very interested in what Zara was doing. Without taking their eyes from her, they whispered and frowned.

Something was clearly going on, but before he could figure out what it was, his mother leaned over and kissed him on the cheek. "It's getting late, so I'm going to retire. I'll put the little boys to bed. You stay up and have fun, son. I love you, and I'm so glad to have you back."

"Love you too, Mom." He watched as she ushered Darius and Petra's young sons out of the room.

He now had a clear view of the couple seated next to his mom. The woman was rubbing the man's crotch while he laughed at something someone was saying. Zara had been right that people were much more open with their sexuality and public displays of affection here.

There was a clatter of dishes behind him. He turned to see yet another young woman picking up a plate. She smiled sweetly at him from under her lashes.

"That is it," Zara mumbled. "How could I have forgotten?" With a swipe of her hand, she cleared a space where his trencher had been and sat on the table in front of him. Grabbing a sweet cake from a nearby platter, she smeared the frosting on the swell of her breasts and gave him a pointed look.

Damn. Public displays weren't his norm, but he was sorely tempted to push her back on the table in front of all these people and slide a hand under her skirts. He felt himself growing hard at the mere thought.

She lifted his chin with one finger. "Work with me."

"You want me to...lick that off?" Movement just over Zara's shoulder caught his eye. A man and woman were sitting in a chair along the back wall. Her skirts covered both of them, and based on how they were moving, they were having sex.

Okay, then.

"Yes," Zara said, her voice husky. "I'm sick of the women here thinking I don't have a claim on you."

"Why would they—?"

"It is customary that a man serves food to his woman and a woman serves food to her man. When we helped ourselves at the beginning of the meal, they just assumed we weren't together."

Thus all the female attention he'd been getting. Now it was his turn to grin at her. "And that made you jealous."

"Yeah, you're damn right I'm jealous."

Snaking his arms around her waist, he buried his face in her breasts and licked the frosting from her creamy skin, his erection straining painfully behind the now-tight leather of his breeches. Strangely, the conversations around them carried on like normal. Call it weird, but he could seriously get into this.

Zara threaded her fingers through his hair. "I want to feel you inside me."

He lifted his head. Right now?

"Yes," she said, correctly reading his unspoken question.

Public sex. So fucking hot.

He cupped her breast and stroked her peaked nipple through layers of fabric. She arched into him, urging him to continue. He glanced around, looking for a quiet corner to have his way with her when he saw Lord D'Angelus approaching.

Damn. They'd have to continue this later. Vince sat back in his seat, licking the frosting from his lips. Zara didn't move, however, and stayed sitting on the edge of the table in front of him.

The older man seemed unfazed. "I hear you're quite a marksman."

Vince frowned. "Who told you that?"

Asher cleared his throat and scooted his chair closer. He had a stupid grin on his face. "I did."

That made no sense. "You haven't seen me shoot."

"No, but Shane and Arlo have."

Was nothing sacred at Reckless? Jeezus. They gossiped like a bunch of old women.

"And your mother said something about you winning a shooting competition," D'Angelus said.

Vince ran a hand through his hair. "For one, mothers

exaggerate. And two, I was a kid. In other words, it was a very long time ago."

"She said you beat out fifty other competitors," D'Angelus said, "mostly adults. I'd hardly call that exaggerating."

As the man took a swig of his ale, Vince cast an exasperated look at Zara. She gave him a saccharine-sweet smile. Apparently, he wasn't going to get any sympathy from her either.

D'Angelus wiped the foam from his mouth with the back of his hand. "Rickert and Asher told me you detected several unknown portals on the way here. Can you show them to the Iron Guild?"

Vince nodded, eager at the change of subject. "Of course. And I found one ten years ago near Zara's family farm." He flicked a glance her way. "How far away is that from here?"

"A good three or four days," she answered.

"Very good then," D'Angelus said. "We'll start the mapping process tomorrow."

CHAPTER EIGHTEEN

Zara had had a few sex dreams before, so when broad hands pushed her legs apart in the middle of the night, she obediently opened them and thought about grabbing the vibrator in her nightstand.

The mattress shifted. Something rough tickled the sensitive skin between her inner thighs. And then, without warning, there was a long, sinful lick.

Ooooh-kaaaaay. Definitely not a dream.

Her new reality came back with a snap. She was in the castle in Cascadia, not her house in Pacifica. In a bedchamber she shared with Vince. Darius was sleeping in a room down the hallway with the other boys.

They were safe. They were together.

She bucked her hips and grabbed at his hair. "Vince!" Her voice echoed through the darkness of the spacious room.

"I woke you," he said softly, as if he was surprised.

Seriously? She would've laughed at the absurdity of those three words if she weren't on the edge of an orgasm already.

He groaned, a deep sound that vibrated against her core. "But I couldn't help it. This is too sweet. I couldn't leave without having a taste of you first."

A flare of panic clawed at her heart.

Leave? He was leaving?

And then she remembered.

He and Asher were going to check out the possible portals he'd sensed on the way here. They would be gone for several days. His absence would only be temporary.

"Relax," he whispered against her, instinctively feeling her tension. "Just enjoy this."

She did as he commanded and her muscles unknotted.

"Mmmm, that's perfect." He slid two fingers inside her—two long, very skillful fingers—and continued that relentless, mind-blowing assault with his tongue.

A powerful orgasm spiraled through her body. Just before it peaked, he slowed down his rhythm. Slower. And slower. And then even slower. Intensifying everything she felt. She clutched at his hair. Cried out and shuddered as he coaxed every last ounce of pleasure from her body.

When he finally withdrew, she sprawled out on the bedclothes, boneless and utterly spent.

Or so she thought.

Vince didn't even give her a chance to catch her breath. "Since you're awake," he rasped, as if that were some sort of explanation for what he was planning to do next.

Moving in slow, fluid motions, he repositioned her beneath him, his large, warm hands on her hips. Then she felt the broad tip of him where his mouth had been a moment earlier. As he pushed into her, he let out a guttural, almost animalistic groan.

Or maybe *she'd* made that sound. She was still so sensitive.

"Holy hell. So slick. So warm." His head fell forward, the veins on his neck bulging. He was watching where they were joined, the expression on his face pure determination as he pounded into her. "So mine."

His possessive declaration thrilled her, which surprised her. She'd been an independent woman for as long as she could remember. No one owned her. And yet she found it incredibly erotic to hear Vince say that she was his.

She hadn't expected to climax again so soon, but there she was again. Shattering into a million quivering pieces as he pulsed into her, roaring his release.

When it was over, he collapsed next to her, swept the

damp hair from her cheek and curled possessively around her.

"Mmmm," she said dreamily. "That was spectacular."

"Yeah, it was," he said, his hand on her belly. "It was thoughts of this that got me through all those dark days."

"Well, that's all behind us now. We have the future together to look forward to."

She felt his body stiffen slightly.

"What's wrong?" she asked.

"Nothing's wrong."

She rolled over to face him. "I can tell that something's bothering you."

He stared at the ceiling and exhaled slowly. "I'm just worried, that's all."

"About what?"

It took him a moment to reply. "I'm not sure I'm what's best for you and Darius."

"What are you talking about?" She propped herself up on one elbow. "You're exactly what we need. You're the man I love and you're Darius's father. He adores you."

"When I see Darius laughing and horsing around with Asher, for instance, I wonder if he'd be better off with a father-figure like that. Someone without all the darkness in their past that I have. Someone who isn't fucked up and tainted."

"You're not, Vince," she said softly, running a hand over his chest.

What kind of bullshit had the doctor put him through to make him question his worth like this? There was no arguing with him when he got this way, but the thought of him leaving one day was almost unbearable. "I wish you didn't have to go on the portal-mapping mission so soon. Can't it wait?"

"The Iron Guild can't afford to let any portals go unguarded," Vince said, a hint of frustration in his tone. "And I detected several on the way here."

"But we just got here. We're not even settled in yet. A few more days aren't going to make a difference."

His mouth tightened. "You're not being fair, Zara. I've got no choice. Keeping you and Darius safe is the most important thing to me. Those portals are unguarded. And there could be more."

Zara slept fitfully and when she woke the next morning, Vince was gone.

She pulled his pillow close and breathed in his masculine scent, regretting how they left things last night.

She got up and checked on Darius, who was busy having fun with Petra's boys—his cousins, he called them—so she had the chamber maid bring in hot water for a long, leisurely bath. When she was done, she went through the stack of clothes that Neyla had given her. She chose a simple, yet beautifully made gray dress, kidskin leather boots and a lacy knit over-vest that hung past her hips.

Zara looked around for a mirror but didn't see one. Everything seemed to fit perfectly, which surprised her a little. Neyla used to be a fashion designer with her own line, so Zara assumed her clothes would be a better fit for skinny girls. But the woman clearly knew how to design clothes that flattered all shapes and sizes.

A few minutes later, she was knocking on Olivia's door. Maybe she had a mirror in her quarters.

"Come in."

She swung open the heavy door to find that Olivia was lacing up a pair of tall boots while Petra paced nervously back and forth. Alexandra and her elderly cousin, whom Zara had met the night before, sat in two upholstered chairs, drinking tea and doing needlepoint, clearly unperturbed by whatever was bothering Petra.

"Am I interrupting something?"

"No, not at all," Olivia replied. "I was just leaving, but Mom and Bettina are staying here if you want to hang out 'til I come back."

Petra was wringing her hands. Something clearly wrong.

"What happened?" she asked.

"One of my boys got hurt," Petra explained. "Down in the barn. We think he broke his leg."

Alexandra chimed in, pride beaming from her

mismatched eyes. "So Olivia, the healer, is going to fix him up."

Zara got a sick feeling in her stomach. "Was Darius with him?"

Petra nodded. "He's the one who ran up to get me. Apparently, the boys were taking turns jumping out of the hayloft."

If this had something to do with that Aerial Deadbeats vlog he was obsessed with, where people post stupid tricks and get hurt doing them, he was going to be in some serious hot water.

When they got to the barn, the boys were gathered around Petra's son, a gangly, golden-skinned boy named Phillip. Olivia laid her hands on him and talked in soothing tones. The boy instantly relaxed as she used her healing Talent on him.

Zara pulled Darius aside. "Okay, young man, what happened?"

"We were just jumping into that pile of hay, and he fell on his leg wrong."

Her hand flew to her chest as she looked up. Holy Fates. The hayloft was at least twenty feet high. "And whose idea was that?"

"They all thought it sounded fun."

Yeah, I'll bet they did. "But whose idea was it?"

Darius pursed his lips and stared at the ground as if trying to decide what to tell her. He'd lied to her about stupid things he'd done before.

"It was my idea, Mom," he said in a flurry of words. "I'm sorry."

She felt a strange mixture of both anger and pride. He'd never 'fessed up like this before. He sounded so grown up. "You're lucky that Aunt Olivia is here to heal him. This isn't like Pacifica where a mobile med-unit can patch you up or you can go to a hospital. Injuries like that—" she inclined her head to where Olivia was helping Phillip to his feet "—can be very serious here."

"Do you think my dad will be disappointed in me?"

She kept her expression solemn even though her heart was bursting. The fact that Vince had already made such an impression on their son was huge. "I'm sure he's not going to be happy about this, but he will be glad to hear that you were honest. Doing the right thing matters deeply to your dad."

She thought back to their conversation the night before. How could Vince feel he wasn't good for Darius? He was exactly what their son needed.

Later in the afternoon, after Olivia had taken a nap to recover from the energy drain, the two women strolled through the market, stopping at many of the vendors in the arts and crafts section. Jewelry. Candles. Textiles. Sculptures. Hand-dyed yarns. Gilded weapons.

Darius ran ahead of them, dragging Alexandra and Bettina toward a colorful tent selling pastries. Or to be more accurate, beignets, given the telltale ring of powdered sugar around Darius's mouth.

It felt strange and foreign to be surrounded by family, like she was living in someone else's skin and had to get used to it, but the feeling was good. Better than she imagined it would be.

She squeezed Olivia's hand. "Thanks for being so tenacious in finding us." Nodding in Darius's direction, she watched him hug his grandmother, his face radiating the same happiness that she was feeling right now. "That, right there, means the world to me."

Olivia smiled, her mismatched eyes crinkling at the corners. "I could say the same about you. My mother is over the moon with joy. Look at her. She got her son and a grandson all in one day."

As they walked through the market, Zara thought about how different this lifestyle and its customs were, but at the root of it all, these were her people and everything fit nicely like a comfortable old shoe. She caught a whiff of curry and spices coming from one of the food vendors several rows away. Yeah, she was definitely home.

"It's such a joy to finally be truthful to Darius about his heritage, when, for so long, I couldn't say a word."

"Why did you move over there in the first place?" Olivia asked. "Was it hard, just the two of you living in what had to be such a strange land?"

The Dynamic Duo, she'd called herself and Darius. Able to do anything by themselves.

Zara sighed. "Vince had told me a lot about what life

was like, so it wasn't a total shock. At the time, I didn't have any ties to keep me here. Asher was who-knew-where, and our mother…" Her voice trailed off and she forced herself to continue. "The sisters took me in, which is where I developed a love of history, particularly the old relics. There are some amazing and fascinating stories. When I heard the sisters lamenting over the fact that they'd located a priceless artifact in Pacifica but didn't know how to retrieve it, I offered to steal it back."

Olivia laughed. "And what was their reaction?"

"Pretty much that," Zara replied with a rueful smile. "They thought I was crazy. So I spent the next few months honing my cloaking skills and learning martial arts to prove to them that I was capable."

"Did Mariah help?" Olivia asked, cocking an eyebrow.

"Ha. Of course."

"Doesn't surprise me. Asher calls her a ninja nun."

Zara laughed. "A fitting description. When I got over there, Mariah introduced me to a former lover who taught me how to pick just about any lock."

That wasn't the only former fling of the woman's that Zara had met. There was the baker who'd taught Zara how to use a modern kitchen. It was his recipe Zara had been using for the cupcakes. And then there was the marine mechanic, a dark-skinned man with white tribal tattoos, who had taught her how to drive.

"Picking locks is a nice skill for a thief to have," Olivia teased. "Were you scared the first time?"

"Petrified and exhilarated."

The first item she'd stolen wasn't the one the sisters had been talking about. It was a jewel-encrusted broach in someone's private collection, which dated back to the time period just after the Obsidian Wars, when the Fates had divided the worlds. She immediately recognized its historical value when its owner, a wealthy library benefactor, brought the piece in to find out more about it. When she learned it would soon be sold at a fundraising auction, she was able to secure an invitation. It had been a simple matter to slip out, grab the relic while cloaked, and tuck it into her handbag. "Had the piece sold, who knew where it would've ended up?"

It had been such a rush. Every time was actually, and she loved it.

She made a mental note to talk to the sisters and let them know that even though her situation was different now, she still wanted to help.

Olivia stopped to examine a small silver box on a table with other trinkets. Lowering her voice, she said, "How do you get the items back through the portal?" Pacificans were known to sacrifice one of their own, ordering some poor, unsuspecting newbie to carry dense metal objects through the portals, which got them killed.

Zara shrugged. "That's Mariah's job. Maybe she's immune to portal sickness, but I don't know for sure."

Olivia turned the object over in her hand. "Or she's got a Healer-Talent waiting for her on the other side."

Zara recalled how Olivia had made her own iron sickness disappear. "That's possible, too."

The other woman was quiet for a moment before speaking up again. "Do you think you could introduce me to the sisters? I'd like to learn more about what they do. Maybe there's something I can do to help."

A thrill ran through her. She and Olivia both working with the sisters? Now that would be one hell of a Dynamic Duo.

"Of course," she replied. There were several *Taghta* abbeys in Cascadia, but she was only familiar with the one near Vallenberg. The one that had taken her in when she had nowhere else to turn.

Sadness pricked her heart as thoughts of her mother flooded her head. The person who should be the most excited for her return didn't even know she was back.

They stopped at a stall selling jewelry, and a crystal pendant caught her eye. Nothing like a little shopping to help a hurting heart.

"Can I see that one?" she asked, pointing. "The third one from the left."

"Ye are drawn to it, eh?" The merchant, a wisp of a woman with sharp, angular features and a colorful headscarf, pulled it from the display and handed it to her.

Strung on a thin leather cord, the filigreed pendant had no front or back, with each side as equally detailed as the other. In the center was a milky white stone. Probably a moonstone. Cascadian magistrates were said to carry them in their pockets to help them understand both sides of a dispute and make the right decision.

"Hold it up to the light, lass," the shopkeeper said. "With yer left hand."

She did so and the stone seemed to glow from within, illuminating thin, current-like swirls in its depths.

"It will bring out a person's psychic abilities. If ye have any," she added, as if she knew somehow that Zara was a Talent. "It will also trap negative energy and help with yer heart's desire."

That was quite a laundry list. "Is that so?"

She bartered the woman down to what she felt was a reasonable amount. After paying, Zara put on the necklace. The pendant hung just past the apex of her breasts, picking up some of the pale apricot from the lacy vest she wore.

The woman tilted her head slightly, stared at Zara's chest, then declared, "It suits ye. Very much."

She wasn't sure what that meant, but she nodded just the same.

The woman turned her attention to Olivia. "And

what can I find for ye, lass? An amber wand perhaps? To help with healing?"

Ah. So the woman *had* divined their Talents.

"Nothing for me, thank you."

Reentering the crowd of people without jostling anyone was like double-dutch jump roping. You had to time it just right and quickly make your move.

"Which way did they go?" Zara asked, walking on her tiptoes in an attempt to see over the man in front of her.

"I'm not sure. Mom said something about Bettina wanting to win a prize for Darius, so maybe they're headed to one of the game booths."

They rounded the corner, heading into the food section of the market, and she heard a familiar voice. One that she hadn't heard for many years, and it made her skin crawl.

She halted, spun around and ducked back the way they'd come.

Olivia was right behind her. "Whoa. What's wrong?"

Her heart beat loudly in her ears. "My stepfather. He's here."

"That asshole?" Olivia balled her hands into fists. Asher must have told her some of the stories of how the man used to beat them for the most ridiculous reasons. His own drunkenness being the most common. "Where?"

Zara jabbed a thumb behind her. "Sitting outside that

pub around the corner, smoking a prath hookah with a few other men."

Olivia stepped out onto the walkway and craned her neck in that direction. "The tall, skinny one or the chubby bald one?"

"The chubby bald one."

"So that's the schmuck that you and Asher dealt with growing up."

"Yep. In the flesh." She thought about the time he'd locked her out in the barn, forcing her to sleep in a stall on one of the coldest nights of the year simply because she couldn't refill his tankard of ale on account of the keg being empty.

"Does this mean your mother is here somewhere too?"

Zara bit her lip and thought about the possibility. Could her mother be here somewhere with the kids? Her half-siblings would have to be in their teens by now. Were they even still living at home? She peered around the corner just in time to see her stepfather ogling the pretty waitress's ample behind.

"He may have left her at home to take care of the farm. Chances are, he's here by himself, drinking and smoking with his buddies."

"Want me to go find out for sure?"

Zara's eyes widened. "And how are you going to do that?"

Olivia held up a finger. "I've got an idea." She

unfastened the top button of her bodice and slipped out one shoulder. Then she loosened her hair and dabbed a sample of rouge from a nearby vendor onto her lips. "Mmmm, nice," she said, smoothing her lips together to distribute the color. "I'll have to come back and buy some of this. How do I look?"

"You are not going to do what I think you're going to do, are you?"

Olivia winked. "Watch and learn."

Zara tried not to gape as her friend made her way through the crowd and stopped in front of the pub. Smoke from several hookah pipes swirled around her. She frowned, appeared to be lost, an expression of confusion flitting across her face. One of the men said something. She turned toward him and laughed. The man grinned and so did Zara's stepfather. They spoke for another minute, Olivia twisting her hair provocatively, nodding and pointing toward who-knew-what. Finally, she gave a little wave and then disappeared into the crowd.

When she didn't show up right away, Zara wondered if she'd truly gotten lost. Finally, ten minutes later, she reappeared at Zara's side, a colorful headscarf wrapped around her hair, its lacy ends tapering down her back.

"Sorry that took so long. There are so many people, I had a hard time making my way back."

"I see you got waylaid at one of the textile vendors," Zara said with a smirk.

Olivia twisted a finger around a strand of hair that had come loose. "Like it?"

"Very pretty. Makes you look sweet and innocent. Like someone on a religious pilgrimage."

That drew a laugh from her friend.

"So, what did my ogre of a stepfather say?"

"A lot of disgusting things, actually. You're right, he really is an ass."

Yeah, not surprising.

"Your mom isn't here," Olivia continued softly. "He didn't bring her."

Zara tamped down her disappointment. At least she knew now that there'd be no chance of running into her. But secretly, she'd hoped her mother was here so that they could talk when her stepfather was busy getting drunk with his friends. "And how did you find that out?"

"I asked them point blank if their women were with them. He was the first one to pipe up with the fact that he'd left his wife at home."

Zara frowned. "Isn't that a little random for a stranger to be asking?"

"Not when you tell them you're looking for the brothel tent because you're one of the new girls."

Zara snorted with laughter and clamped a hand over her mouth. "Oh my Fates. You didn't."

Olivia grinned. "I told them if they stopped by later that I'd give them a special deal."

Zara's stomach hurt from laughing so hard. "You are going to have to pay me big time not to tell Asher."

Olivia rolled her eyes. "Please. He'd probably find it hot. Actually, not *probably*. I *know* he'd find it hot. He's into role-playing and stuff."

"Oh really? Do tell."

"Nope," the other woman laughed. "My lips are sealed."

It was late afternoon by the time they finally caught up with the others. Alexandra and Bettina were sitting in the shade of a large tree. Phillip had joined them at some point, and he and Darius were at a nearby game tent, taking turns aiming a giant slingshot at a target in an attempt to win a prize.

If Vince were here, she could picture him coaching Darius. She wondered what he was doing right now, wishing they hadn't left things the way that they had.

Zara took a place on the rug and waved over a young girl selling glasses of *ogappa* cider. "Wow, Phillip looks great."

"Hard to believe the boy had a broken leg a few hours ago," Alexandra said.

Bettina agreed.

Olivia frowned as she watched the boys. "He really should be taking it easy. The bone is mended, but it'll probably hurt tonight with all this activity."

Alexandra patted her daughter's hand. "Well, don't

go healing him again. You've done plenty already. It takes too much out of you."

"I know, Mom. I won't." She threw Zara a sidelong glance.

Once a mom, always a mom, Zara imagined her saying. It made her think about her mom again. She was back at the farm, while jerk-face was here. It was a three- maybe four-day ride away.

The girl arrived with a tray filled with tall, thin glasses of cider. Bettina insisted on paying.

Zara took a long sip. She'd forgotten how good the sweet, tangy drink was. "Alexandra, what would you think if I took Darius and went to visit my mother for a few days? Would you be terribly upset?" Without going into many details, she explained that her stepfather was here and that she hadn't seen her mother in years. "It would be nice to see her without him around. Plus, she's never met Darius."

"You don't want to wait for Vince to come back?" Alexandra asked, furrowing her brow.

"I'm not sure how long my stepfather will be here. I can't imagine he'll stay for the Games. He's...uh...not exactly a fan." She lowered her voice. "The portal Vince came through is very near my childhood home. He'll be showing that to Asher, so they'll be going that way soon anyway. If you let them know where I am, we can ride back together."

She and her mother had once been close. Maybe she

could give Zara some perspective on how to deal with what was going on between her and Vince. She'd once been married to a proud man.

"Do you mind if I come with Asher and Vince?" Olivia asked. "Then you can show me that place we were talking about."

"Or you can just come with us."

Olivia narrowed her eyes. "You don't want to spend time alone with your mom?"

Zara appreciated her friend's concern. "I'm sure she'd want to meet the woman her son loves. Plus, we could stop in and see the sisters at the abbey near Vallenberg. See what we can do to help them. Besides, I'd love the company on the ride there."

Olivia turned to Alexandra. "Are you okay with that, Mom?"

The older woman waved her hand. "I'll be fine, honey. You go. This is important."

And then it was settled. Zara, Darius and Olivia would leave first thing in the morning.

CHAPTER NINETEEN

*V*ince should've been ecstatic. Together with Asher, he'd found three previously unknown portals around Crestenfahl. One location was no more than a small fissure in the rock, but the other two were viable. Asher had presented Vince's discoveries at a hastily called meeting with the Iron Guild members on hand for the Games. They were so impressed that they called for him to speak to them directly. As he pointed out the various locations on a map spread out on the table and how he'd been able to detect them, there were many oohs and ahhs. Some whispers.

But as he spoke, he couldn't help thinking about Zara and how much he missed her. She'd been gone when he'd arrived back at the castle. As Asher called the warriors together, Vince had scoured the castle for her, finally running into his mother who told him that Zara, Darius and Olivia had left.

Unease prickled the back of his neck that she'd gone off to Vallenberg on her own. As Asher talked to the group, Vince couldn't sit still. He paced back and forth, feeling unsettled that he wasn't with Zara and Darius to protect them if they should need him. He hadn't liked how things had been left between them. Was that why she hadn't waited for him? Because she didn't know if he'd be there to count on in the long run?

After the meeting was over, Asher pulled him aside. "Nice work, bro."

Vince tried to duck the compliment. "Yeah, well—"

Asher knocked him in the arm. "I'm serious. I've never seen that sort of reaction from them. You did good. I wouldn't be surprised if they petitioned the leadership to extend you an invitation to join the Guild as a warrior."

Vince was stunned. No way. Join the Iron Guild? "Are you serious?"

Asher nodded. "Even Rickert agrees. And if that doesn't happen, one of us could sponsor you and get the Guild to vote."

They would stake their professional reputations for him? Vince exhaled slowly and thought about what it would be like being a Warrior of the Iron Guild. Did he dare dream that could actually happen? It'd be a chance to join his friends and fight their common enemy together. But would Zara be on board? Her own father had been killed in the line of duty.

God, he wished she were here so they could lay in bed, wrapped up in each other's arms, and talk about all the possibilities. With this life-changing opportunity as an Iron Guild warrior, maybe he could finally let go of the past and feel worthy of Zara's love and devotion. Be the kind of father that Darius could really look up to.

He loved her more than he ever thought possible— both her and Darius—and couldn't imagine life without them. He'd been a fool to think he could ever walk away from them.

Asher smacked him on the back, jerking him from his thoughts. "Let's go grab a cold one down in the market. Drown out our sorrow that the women are gone. Then we'll leave for Vallenberg tomorrow. If we don't lollygag, we might even be able to catch up with them before they get there."

Vince bit back a smile. Lollygag? "No looking for portals on the way there?"

"You're not the only one who misses his woman," Asher said with a knowing smirk. "Let's ride straight there, then on the way back, we'll map any others you detect."

Good plan. That way, Darius would be with them. Based on his son's reactions, he had a feeling the boy had been born with the same Talent. It may not be fully manifested yet, but he did seem to have a sense for them. He could test out this theory with Darius on the way back.

They got to the pub tent and found an open table in the back.

"Order me some of that lamb stew and an ale, would you?" Asher asked. "I won't be long."

Vince frowned. "Where are you going?"

Asher rubbed the back of his neck. "I…uh…ordered a ring for Olivia from a jewelry maker around the corner. I'm going to check to see if it's ready yet."

"An engagement ring?" He was confused. Weren't they already engaged?

Asher nodded, his eyes glittering with excitement. "I proposed to her without one. I hope she'll like it."

Vince scoffed. "Of course she'll love it. But then, seeing how she worships the ground you walk on, you could use a piece of twine as an engagement ring and she'd think it was beautiful." He rolled his eyes. "It's kind of nauseating, actually."

"Fuck you, mate," Asher said, laughing. "And keep your filthy hands off my stew if it gets here before I do. Or you'll be sorry."

Vince held up his hands. "Don't worry. I have no plans to touch your meat."

After Asher had left, a harried but efficient waitress took his order and quickly returned with a tankard of ale. Vince leaned back in his chair, took a long draught and surveyed the place. Dimly lit by several rustic candelabras hanging from wooden support beams, the tent was packed and loud. Every table filled. He and Asher were lucky to have found this one. The din of so many people talking and laughing nearly drowned out the sound of a man playing a mandolin near the bar. For the first time in ages, he was finally beginning to feel settled and content. At peace, even.

The waitress flitted past him again, carrying a tray of food to a nearby table. The smell of onions, spices and cooked meat wafted over him like a heavenly cloud. No wonder the place was packed and Asher invoked that threat. The smell was like a calling card to any red-blooded, meat-loving male who happened to be in the vicinity.

He drained his ale as platter after platter of food was delivered to other patrons until finally the waitress returned to his table with two steaming bowls of stew and thick slices of bread. Screw Asher, he thought as he grabbed a spoon. He was too hungry to be polite right now and wait for the guy.

The tent flap opened and a cold gust of air blew his napkin off the table. He bent to pick it up and glanced at the door to see if it was Asher. If it was, he was going to pretend to be digging into the guy's food. But it wasn't Asher. It was a large beast of a man.

Vince squinted. There was something vaguely familiar about the guy, but in the dim light, he couldn't see the details of his face.

He turned his attention back to his stew and shoveled in a bite. The meat, potatoes and gravy melted in his mouth. He stuffed in another bite and another. He hadn't realized how hungry he was, although he had a feeling that even if he wasn't hungry, he could still eat a boatload of this stuff.

"How is it?" Asher asked, taking the seat opposite him. He wasted no time digging in.

"Freaking awesome." Coming up for air, Vince took a long sip of ale and looked over at his friend. His future brother-in-law. "So, did you get it?"

Asher didn't look up. "No, it won't be ready for a few more days."

"Guess you'll have that to look forward to when we get back from Vallenberg." With the spoon halfway to his mouth, he paused when the back of his neck prickled.

He glanced toward the opening of the tent and then around bar. The man from earlier was staring at him. And this time Vince could see his face.

He blinked, not sure if what he was seeing was accurate. The guy looked exactly like Sean from the Institute.

Vince lowered his hand slowly as the realization hit him. This guy *was* Sean.

Sean shook his head slightly and slanted a glance at the door. Through the gap in the tent, he could see a few men standing just outside.

He took his spoon and tapped it against Asher's bowl. "Hey."

The other man looked up, an irritated expression on his face. If he were a dog eating his food, he would've growled.

Vince dropped his voice. "Something's wrong. Can you watch the door? Make sure those guys don't get in."

Asher cranked his head around to get a look. "What's going on?"

"That man. The big one near the bar. He was a fellow prisoner with me in the Institute."

Asher cursed under his breath. "What the fuck is he doing here?"

"That's what I'm going to find out. Make sure those men don't come in. If they are who I think they are, they may recognize me, but they won't know who you are."

And with that, he pushed himself from the table and strode over to Sean.

Before Vince could ask the guy what the hell was going on, Sean blurted, "Vince, I'm sorry. They threatened my family."

"What the fuck are you talking about, Sean?"

"The doctor. He threatened my little girl. He took me in his private limo to a playground where she was with her friends. Said he'd kill her if I didn't cooperate." The big man closed his eyes briefly, a war of emotion playing out on his face. "I had no choice but to agree to find you."

Vince's nostrils flared and he gritted his teeth. "With my tracking chip?" Sean had helped him cut it out from under his skin. How was that even possible?

The former inmate shook his head. "I'm a Tracker-Talent. As soon as the Impedio wore off, they brought me through the portal. I detected you a few days ago."

Vince tried to keep his fist from smashing into the guy's face. "How many came through the portal?"

Sean glanced nervously behind him. "If they see me talking to you—"

"They won't. My friend will see to that. Now talk."

"There were ten men who came through the portal with me."

His jaw ticked. "What portal?"

"They kept me blindfolded on the way there, but the doctor kept calling it Crawford's Portal."

The Vallenberg portal? It felt as if he'd been punched in the stomach. That was the one near Zara's home. How had they found it? He hadn't told the doctor anything.

"Are they all here with you in Crestenfahl?"

"There are six of us, including me. Two outside that door and I'm not sure where the other three are. Somewhere around the market, I guess. I...I told them I thought my signals were getting confused with all these people here and that I needed to sit down to rest."

Six in Crestenfahl. That left four more. "You said ten came through the portal. Where are the others?"

"Back at the farm. Arrangements were made with the farmer there. They were using it as their headquarters."

Panic reached down inside Vince, wrapped its tendrils around his heart and squeezed.

Zara's family farm was the closet to the portal. Did her stepfather make a deal with them? From what Zara and Asher had told him about the guy, it wasn't outside the realm of possibilities.

"And Vince?"

His eyes snapped up and met Sean's. There was a deep sadness reflected there.

"One of them is the doctor."

CHAPTER TWENTY

*T*his had to be the girl from the drawings. Had to be.

The doctor tried to contain his excitement as he walked in a circle around her, examining her from every angle. She was tied to a support beam in the barn, so she wasn't going anywhere.

She'd arrived a short time ago with the boy. His men had stopped them on the road coming in. She'd protested all their questions, saying she was the daughter of the woman who lived on this farm and that she had *every damn right* to be here. When Uri heard her name, he couldn't believe his good fortune. She'd scratched and clawed, put up quite a fight, but she was no match for his men.

Shortly after appearing on Birdie Lyon's show, he'd done some digging of his own. The so-called accomplice

Birdie had referred to, the woman she believed had helped Vincent escape, was named Zara. Not exactly a common name.

It all fell into place now. Vincent had come through the portal as a horny young teenager and began having sex with a girl from a nearby farm. And then he got her pregnant. Although Uri wasn't sure that Vincent had known about the boy. He hadn't mentioned anything about him while under the effects of the drug. Just the woman and the portal.

But how had this woman helped him escape? She didn't look formidable at all. Sure, Palmer, the overseer, was incompetent, but there had to be more.

His gnarled hands shook, and he absently tugged at the neckline of his borrowed tunic.

She had a pretty face and shiny, dark hair, so he understood why Vincent had been attracted to her. But to go through what he had in order to protect her?

Uri glanced over at the boy sitting on an overturned milking bucket where one of his men was standing guard. So this was Vincent Crawford's son. Was he a Talent like his father? Could he find portals, too, or did he have another ability? A thrill ran down his spine at what this would mean for his research.

"Hey," the woman said, her eyes dark and menacing.

She was clearly trying to draw his attention away from the boy. A mother instinctively knew when her child was in danger. An admirable quality, he had to admit, though pointless under these circumstances.

"What did you do to my mother?" she demanded.

Uri pointed in the direction of the farmhouse. "She's fine. We're guests here."

Her face twisted into a harsh, unattractive expression. "What are you talking about?"

"Let's just say we made a mutually beneficial arrangement with her husband."

"With Henry?"

Nodding, the doctor paced to the double doors and back. "Henry provides us with clothing at the portal, a place to stay, transportation. And in turn, we pay him handsomely. It's a good arrangement."

Her eyes narrowed to small, crescent-moon slits. "My stepfather is helping Pacificans sneak into Cascadia?" She made a derisive sound. "That shouldn't surprise me, but it does. I didn't think anyone here could stoop that low."

"Greed is a powerful motivator. As long as you cooperate with us, no harm will come to you either."

"Why do you need my cooperation? Or do I even want to know?"

He turned to face her and watched her closely. "You were Vincent Crawford's girl, weren't you?"

It was as if he'd just thrown cold water into her face. Her cheeks reddened and she clamped a hand over her gaping mouth.

He wanted to laugh at how completely taken by surprise she was. For the first time, he understood why Birdie Lyons did what she did. Seeing someone react to a shocking revelation without warning was a goddamn adrenaline rush. Even his long-dormant prick twitched.

The woman's expression turned icy. "Then you must be the asshole who imprisoned and tortured him."

"So he told you about me? I'm flattered." He put a hand over his heart. "I've missed him, you know? Our little talks about life and how the world works. We talked quite a bit about you, as a matter of fact. I told him that if you were as perfect as he said you were, then he didn't deserve to be with you. He let his father down, he let his mother and sister down, and he'd eventually let you down."

Her eyes grew even colder. "Liar."

"How do you think I found out about the portal? And how did I know to come here?" He spread his hands wide and looked around. "Vincent told me about your stepfather. The drinking. The violence. How he was going to take you away from all that."

The woman turned her head away quickly, trying to shield her face from him.

"Stop that," the boy blurted out for the first time. "Stop making my mom cry."

He was a handsome young lad. Thick, blond hair. The fresh, plump skin of a child who hadn't lost his baby fat yet.

Uri smiled. "Well, aren't you a brave fellow?"

"When my dad comes—and he will—he and my uncle are going to smash your face in."

No wonder Pacificans called these people barbarians. He paused, frowned and looked at the boy again. Those eyes. So defiant. Just like his father. "Is that so?"

The boy opened his mouth. His mother tried to stop him, but he blurted it out anyway. "Yeah, my uncle is an Iron Guild warrior and my dad knows a bunch of them."

The doctor paced around the barn, tugging at the collar of his scratchy tunic again.

Warriors. Here. On their home turf.

He and his men had a few firearms, having sacrificed a young recruit early on to bring them through the portal, but it wasn't much. They'd purposely kept a low profile as they quietly tried to fit in. Using Pacifican weapons would've drawn attention to the fact that they weren't from here.

He was so deep in thought that he hadn't been watching where he was going. Something squished beneath his boots. He looked down.

Oh for Pete's sake.

He'd stepped in a pile of horse manure. Both boots.

These were the only pair he had, having borrowed them from Henry. He tried to smear it off by scuffing the soles on the ground, but shit still clung to the edges.

God, he hated this place.

The seed of an idea began to take shape. Maybe he

didn't need to stick around here to get Vincent after all. Uri's benefactor back in Pacifica had what he wanted— access to Cascadia without the army's knowledge. And now that the doctor had both the woman *and* the son in his clutches, Vincent would be forced to come to him. He'd have to cooperate. Just as Sean had.

If they left now, he'd be able to sleep in his own bed tonight. He quickly barked out orders. "Untie her. Bring the boy. Get our things together. We're leaving."

"Without the others?" one of his men asked.

"They're big boys. They'll figure out we left when they come back and find us gone." Most were his benefactor's men anyway and they had their own agenda.

"Where are you taking us?" the woman demanded.

The doctor smiled. "To the other side. Back to *my* home turf, where *I* have the advantage."

"Both of us?" Zara asked, panic making her voice high-pitched. "You don't need to bring him. All you need is me."

"Mom, no!" the boy cried.

The doctor laughed. "Don't worry, son. I'm not separating you from your mother. Having both of you will make it impossible for your father to refuse to cooperate. Something he's quite good at doing, which has been a source of much frustration for me, I will admit."

"Why do you need Vince?" she asked, her eyes pleading. "What is so important about his cooperation?"

"He can find portals."

"That's why the *army* wants him. Why do *you* want him? What did Vince ever do to you?"

Anger heated his veins. "Because it's my job to break Talents. Get them to work for the army whether they want to or not. And I get upset when I can't do my job."

"Do you hate Cascadians so much that you want to see us destroyed?" she asked, her voice wavering. "What did we ever do to you?"

"It's not that I hate Cascadians, Ms. Kane. At least, not as much as some do. The thing is…" An image of his daughter flashed in his mind—her unseeing stare, her shell of a body. "I hate Talents."

CHAPTER TWENTY-ONE

They'd ridden all day and all night, switching horses a few times at villages along the way. About an hour away from Vallenberg, a heavy unease fell over Vince as if invisible fingers were squeezing his heart. He was riding next to Asher, trying to figure out whether to go to the abbey first or head straight to the farm. Vince's mother had told them that Zara, Olivia and Darius were going to be stopping at both places.

Asher was saying they should swing by the abbey first, since it wasn't too far off the main road. But Vince wasn't listening to him, consumed instead by the strange sensation.

"Oh man," he said, loosening his hold on the reins and rubbing at the hollowness inside his chest.

Asher slowed his horse. "What's wrong? Are you all right?"

"I'm...I'm not sure," Vince replied. "It's not me, though."

"Then what is it?"

It had something to do with Zara. He was positive.

"It's Zara. She's in trouble."

"What?" Asher snapped. "Are you sure? How do you know?"

"I...I don't know how. I just do. One moment she's there, you know, taking up space in my heart, and the next minute...I can't feel her anymore."

"Shit, man." Exhaling roughly, Asher scrubbed a hand over his face.

She was in great danger. All three of them were.

He and Asher spurred the horses on. His only hope was that the women had stopped at the abbey first and hadn't yet been to the farm.

When they arrived, they veered onto a path that took them to a hill overlooking the small valley. There, they could observe what was going on without being seen. But when they dismounted and crept to the top of the hillside, his worst fears came true. The first thing he saw was Zara's chestnut mare grazing in a nearby field.

Asher cursed. "They did come here first."

The thought of Zara and Darius—the two people on earth he loved more than life itself—in the presence of pure evil was enough to drive Vince mad with rage. He didn't care what it would take or what he'd have to do, he was going to get to them.

He started to charge down the hillside, but Asher grabbed him by the shoulder and hauled him back.

"What the fuck?" Asher had no idea what kind of a man the doctor was, but he sure as hell did. "We need to get to them *now*."

"We must be careful," he said, pointing to a man stationed outside the barn. "We have to assume they brought firearms through the portal."

"Okay. Guns. Got it."

They made their way down the hillside on foot, staying hidden in the trees. When they got to the backside of the barn, they split up.

When Vince came around the barn, Asher had a man in a headlock.

"I swear," the guy choked, trying to break Asher's hold on his neck. "There were only two of them. A woman named Zara and a young boy."

"Where are they now?" Vince asked through gritted teeth.

"They left with Dr. Dobrynin and his bodyguard about an hour ago. They were going to the portal."

With a punch to the jaw, it was lights out for the guy.

"Come on," Vince barked after they hogtied him securely in the barn. "Let's go."

"Since Olivia wasn't with them," Asher said, "I've got to find her first. She must've gone to the abbey to give Zara and Darius a chance to visit with Mom alone."

"Then I'm going by myself. I can't wait." He couldn't

stand the thought that Zara and Darius were with the doctor. One minute with that lunatic was one minute too long.

Asher ran a hand over his thin braids and grimaced. "You can't do this, Vince. It could be a trap. The doctor's men could be waiting for you on the other side."

"Well, I'm not going to take the time to go all the way to one of the portals we mapped on the other side of Crestenfahl. That would take days."

Asher grabbed him by the shoulders. "It's suicide."

Vince tried to jerk away from Asher, but the man held tight. "Let go of me."

"Vince, if you wait, we can round up some other men and—"

He wanted Vince to wait?

There was no way in hell he was waiting. He tried getting away again, but Asher held on with an iron grip. Fuck, the guy was strong.

"I get that you want to help them, but how is walking into a trap going to do that?"

Anger clawed at him. He could almost feel it bursting through his skin. But before he could tell his friend to fuck off again, the air around them rumbled.

"What is that?" Asher said.

"I...I don't know. It feels like this when there's a portal nearby."

"The one the doctor knows about?"

"No," Vince said, confused. He looked around, not

sure what he was feeling. But a portal was definitely calling to him. A different one. "I think I may have just opened up another portal."

"Holy Fates," Asher said, letting go of Vince. "That's insane, bro."

"Yeah, I know. But I'm positive that's what it is."

Asher exhaled. "I'm going to make sure Olivia is safe at the abbey, then I'll come help. Will the portal stay open or is it temporary?"

Vince shrugged, never taking his eyes off a ripple in the air about thirty feet away. "Guess I'll find out."

WHEN ZARA CAME TO, she was lying on the floor in a pitch-black room, her head pounding. All she wanted to do was curl up into a tiny ball and go back to sleep, but a sound kept cutting through the haze. She tried her best to ignore it, but it kept getting louder and louder. And now someone was shaking her arm.

"Stop," she mumbled. "Just stop."

"Mom, please wake up." It was Darius.

And then it all came crashing back to her.

The doctor. The needle. The struggle in the barn. She'd been drugged.

In the dim light, she could see her son kneeling in front of her. "Darius, are you okay?"

"I'm scared, Mom."

Her arms were weak, but she still managed to pull her baby boy into a mama-bear hug. No one was going to hurt him or take him away from her. She'd kill anyone who tried.

He returned the hug, squeezing tight. "I wasn't sure if you were going to ever wake up."

"I'm sorry, honey. They gave me some medicine that made me sleep." She noticed that both of them were wearing thin cotton shifts. The kind you'd see in a hospital. "Do you know where we are?"

Darius shook his head, his lower lip quivering.

It killed her to see him scared. She brushed the hair out of his face. "They took us through a portal, right?"

"I think so. We rode horses to another cave that made my skin tingle. When we stepped through the wall, people were waiting for us and wrapped us in blankets."

So the doctor had brought them back to Pacifica.

Ignoring the fuzziness in her head, she pushed herself to her feet and looked around. They appeared to be in a low-ceilinged storeroom with stacks of boxes along both walls. Several were marked *Christmas*.

What the hell? They must be in a private home rather than the Institute. She wasn't sure why this fact bothered her, but it did. Maybe because if Vince learned that the doctor had kidnapped them, the first place he'd think to look would be the Institute. The doctor probably knew this too, which was why they were here. Wherever *here* was.

She needed to stem the terror that threatened to consume her and figure out how they were going to get out of here. She rattled the door handle. It was locked, of course, but the door itself didn't seem fortified. It was just an ordinary interior door. What she wouldn't give to have her lock-picking set right now.

Somewhere above them, a door slammed and then they heard footsteps. Someone was approaching.

She bent down to Darius's level. "Honey, I'm going to need you do to exactly as I say, okay?"

He nodded.

"You know how your dad can find portals?"

"Yeah."

"Well, I have a special Talent too that I haven't told you about." She quickly explained what a Cloaking-Talent was. "So when I grab your hand and concentrate, I can make it so that they can't see us. But you'll need to be very quiet, okay? Just don't let go of my hand. When whoever that is comes into the room, we'll slip out behind them. Like little mice. Does that sound like a plan?"

"I think so."

The footsteps got louder. It sounded like there were two people coming this direction.

"Ready, honey? No talking, okay? I won't let go of you, no matter what, so you don't let go of me either."

Darius pursed his lips together and nodded.

Taking his hand, she took a deep breath and centered herself. She'd need to keep them cloaked long enough for her to figure out where they needed to go. Once she did, they'd run like hell.

The footsteps stopped outside the door, and a set of keys jangled.

Something was wrong. She didn't feel the familiar whisper of energy along her arms. They weren't cloaked yet. She concentrated harder. Still nothing.

Panic rose up inside her.

"Mom?"

Holy Fates, why couldn't she do this? She'd cloaked both Vince and herself before. Darius was smaller. It should be easy. Closing her eyes, she dug deep inside, but still came up with nothing.

And then she remembered Vince telling her about Impedio, the drug the doctor used to suppress the Talents of his prisoners. The needle.

A key slid into the lock and the door swung open.

The old doctor walked in. "So glad you're finally awake. We've got a lot to talk about."

CHAPTER TWENTY-TWO

When Vince stepped out of the portal, he was shocked. Not only was he fully clothed with his blade strapped to his hip, but he was standing in a wooded area on the front side of the doctor's home.

Zara was here. He was sure of it. The portal had taken him here.

But he had a sneaking suspicion it was not a permanent portal. By the time Asher got back to the farm with his men, it would be gone. Vince knew he was here on his own.

Just as he was trying to decide how to best get inside, one of the four garage doors slid open. He nearly choked when he saw Zara and Darius being shoved into the backseat of a black limousine. Was it the same one he'd been in ten years ago when the doctor ordered the brutal murder of his father?

He sprinted down the driveway, arms and legs pumping. Without a vehicle, he wouldn't be able to follow them. He couldn't let them leave.

Drawing his weapon, he raced into the garage just in time to see the doctor climb in after them and slam the door shut. He was not going to let the doctor take his woman and child away.

But just as he reached for the door handle, he saw movement out of the corner of his eye. He ducked but he wasn't quick enough. An iron-like fist smashed him in the face and he lost his grip on his weapon. Stumbling, he fell to his knees.

The blows kept coming. One after another. Until he wondered if the man really did have an iron fist.

He pulled himself up to all fours only to be kicked in the gut with a boot, knocking him down to the ground again, the exhaust pipe inches from his face. He choked, rolled into the fetal position, hardly able to breathe. Something pressed against his left ear. It took him only a second to realize that he needed to move. His head was behind the rear tire. If the car was put into reverse, he'd be dead.

Using every ounce of strength he had, he pushed himself up, his hand brushing against the handle of his blade. He grabbed it and darted out of the way just as his attacker was reaching for the driver's door.

He could not let this car leave the garage.

Holding the knife by the tip of the blade, Vince took aim and threw. It hit the man in the back with a thunk, and he fell to the floor of the garage.

Adrenaline surged through him. All that stood between him and his family now was a frail old man.

Suddenly, the car jerked backwards. It shot past him and he saw the doctor's face in the window.

Vince sprinted out of the garage, but he wasn't fast enough. The doctor whipped the limousine around and it sped out of the driveway.

"Noooo!" he shouted as the taillights disappeared around the corner. His heart sank. He had no doubt where the doctor was taking them. They were on their way to the Institute.

He ran back into the garage and checked to see if keys were in any of the other cars. They weren't. He tried the door to the house, hoping maybe there were keys hanging on a hook nearby, but the door was locked.

Just as he was thinking he'd have to check if one of the neighbors left their keys in a car, he noticed a shiny gray coupe parked in the turnaround.

His assailant's car?

He sidestepped the blood pooling around the body, trying not to think about how similar it looked when his father had died, and reached into the man's pocket. A set of keys jangled.

A minute later, he was behind the wheel and racing out of the neighborhood. The doctor had a jump on him, but not for long.

Vince caught up to them on the narrow bridge spanning the high-speed rail lines. If he didn't stop them now, they'd hit the freeway and he'd be forced to follow them all the way to the Institute. Unless the doctor called in the army first.

Jamming his foot on the gas, he sped past the limo, cranked the wheel, and forced the doctor to slam on the brakes. The limo skidded sideways and crashed against the guardrail before coming to an abrupt stop. Smoke billowed from under the crumpled hood.

Vince jumped out of the car just as the doctor did. But the doctor had Darius by the hand and they stood near the edge of the bridge. It was then that Vince noticed the guardrail had been damaged in the crash.

"Give me the keys to that car," the doctor ordered, pieces of his comb-over hanging in his face.

Darius looked terrified, which cut Vince to the core. "Let him go."

"Give me the keys," the doctor repeated, "and I'll let your son live. He'll come with me, but at least he'll be alive. You can have the woman. It's the boy I want."

"What kind of a twisted son of a bitch are you?"

The doctor had Darius by the wrist. "I told you about my daughter." Yes, Vince had heard many times about the woman who'd suffered a traumatic brain injury at the hands of a Mind-Talent when she was a child, leaving her in a permanent vegetative state.

"The young friend who messed up her mind was about the same age as your boy here."

"So you're going to take out your revenge on an innocent child who had nothing to do with what happened to your daughter?"

"I'm not going to stop my research. I don't care if the army pulls the funding, I will not give up. You're abominations. Your Talents should be controlled, and if not, you should be destroyed. All of you."

The door to the limo opened and Zara staggered out. She pointed to the doctor. "Let. Him. Go. And maybe we'll let *you* live."

The wail of several sirens could be heard above the din of the trains below. Vince glanced back and saw the flashing lights.

The doctor smiled, pushed the wisps of hair from his face. "Sounds like you're too late."

"It's never too late where my family is concerned."

Vince lunged for Darius. The doctor jerked him away. But in the process, he lost his footing on the wet pavement and stumbled backward. Trying to catch himself, he grabbed for the broken guardrail with his free hand, but he missed and toppled over the edge. Taking Darius with him.

Zara screamed as Vince shot forward and managed to grab the sleeve of Darius's coat. The doctor, still hanging onto Darius's other hand, dangled over the edge. But the borrowed coat was too big. Darius was slipping.

"Dad!"

With a grunt, Vince leaned over the edge as far as he could and clamped a hand around the boy's wrist. "I've got you, son. I won't let go." However, at this angle, he struggled to get leverage and haul Darius up. The doctor was dead weight.

"Face it, Vincent," the doctor rasped from below. "Your son is going to die because of you."

Movement to his right caught his attention.

Zara was holding the neck of a champagne bottle she'd retrieved from the back of the limo. She reached over the guardrail, took aim and dropped it.

There was a loud thunk. A cry of pain.

And then the weight pulling at Darius was gone.

Vince hauled his son back over the guardrail as the doctor fell to the railroad tracks below.

Zara rushed over to them, and with Darius clinging to his neck, Vince fiercely embraced his family.

"Dad, you saved me," Darius mumbled, his arms and legs wrapped around Vince like a monkey.

Zara lifted her face to his, eyes glistening with tears. "You came for us, just like I knew you would."

He kissed her tenderly, tasting the salt of her tears. Then he kissed the top of Darius's sweaty head.

His whole world was right here in his arms.

CHAPTER TWENTY-THREE

*S*everal *months later.*

At daybreak on the top of Red Mountain, a small group of people gathered for the Iron Guild induction ceremony. The air was thick with anticipation. No one said a word as a cool wind blew around them and thunder rumbled ominously in the distance.

With a hand on Darius's back, Zara watched in awe as a monk in black robes presented Vince with a gorgeous blade made from cold-forged Balkirk steel. Eyes cast downward, Vince rose from his kneeling position, nodded once and took the weapon. Asher, his sponsor, stood behind him, a solemn and respectful expression on his face. The time for partying would come later.

Olivia stood next to Zara, holding Alexandra's hand

as the older woman silently wept. They were as proud of Vince as Zara was.

The monk went down the line and presented the other inductees with their Iron Guild weapons, but Zara couldn't tear her gaze from Vince. Behind him, the sun rose like a phoenix over distant peaks, silhouetting his handsome profile.

How fitting, she thought, pride swelling behind her breastbone. Her man was a warrior. Undaunted by challenges. He was strong, fearless, determined. He'd risen from the ashes of his past to face a future filled with hope.

And she loved him with every fiber of her being.

She breathed deeply the crisp air of Cascadia and said a silent prayer of thanks to the Fates. They'd opened up a portal that led Vince to her, and they'd opened up another one that brought him back to her.

Her hand went unconsciously to her belly. She hoped he wouldn't be too surprised by what she would be telling him later. But what did he expect? They'd spent a lot of time in bed since they'd been in Cascadia. Making up for lost time, he'd told her.

She just wished it hadn't happened so soon. Vince already had an instant family to get used to without adding another child to the mix. Not to mention a new home, a new job, new friends. It was a lot for anyone to take in at one time. She'd been thinking about opening up her own bakery here, but that would have to wait a little longer. Family came first.

By the time they got back to Crestenfahl, the party was already in full swing. Seemed the whole village was celebrating the induction of the newest members of the Iron Guild. Given all the activity, you'd have thought the games were still going on.

"Dad, can I go look at my puppy again?"

"Sure, son," Vince said. "But if they're sleeping, don't disturb them."

"Okay."

Conry had fathered a litter of pups and Darius had talked them into letting him have one. They'd be weaned next week.

"Have you decided on a name for him?"

Darius gave them a serious look. "Not yet. Mom is going to take me to the *Taghta* sisters so I can look through their history books. I want him to have a Cascadian name."

The instant they stepped through the gates, Darius ran off with his friends, Conry on his heels.

Inside the great hall of the castle, several minstrels were playing a lively tune. Couples had paired off in a large circle. It was a folk dance she'd learned as a girl.

But before she could reach for Vince's hand and show him the steps, Asher came up and wanted to talk to him. They stood near the wall about ten feet away, deep in conversation, but every few seconds, he'd glance at her, and she knew she was foremost on his mind.

She looked around the room and wondered if her father's induction ceremony into the Iron Guild had been like this. And then she thought about her mother. With her stepfather in custody and awaiting trial by the magistrates, Zara wished her mother had accepted Asher's invitation to come to the castle, but she'd politely refused.

"Give her time," Asher's mother had told her, and that had made Zara smile. She was good at being patient.

A warm hand cupped the nape of her neck. "Let's get out of here," Vince ordered.

"Don't you think we should stay a little longer? Mingle? At least make more than a two minute appearance?"

His hand slipped down to rest possessively on her breast. "No," he said simply. "I want you all to myself."

"But—"

"Don't argue with me, Zara. You looked amazing today on the mountain. I've been waiting too long as it is." His long fingers rubbed her nipples through the fabric and heat surged between her legs. "Unless, of course, you'd like to engage in some public displays of affection right here. Although I'll warn you," he said with a smirk, "I'm talking about more than just kissing."

Before she knew what was happening, Vince swept

her into his arms and carried her through the crowd. The whistles and catcalls came from all around them.

"Retiring so soon?"

"Don't do anything I wouldn't do. Which isn't much."

"Be sure to sheath that sword first."

She tucked her head into his shoulder. Embarrassed. But not really. These were her people—their people—and she loved them.

As he climbed the stairs, she figured now was as good a time as any to break the news to him. His reddish-brown hair was longer now, and she brushed it away from his cheek.

"I have something to tell you."

"Whatever it is," he growled, "it's going to have to wait. There's only one thing I'm in the mood for and it sure as hell isn't talking."

He wasn't kidding either. When they got to their room, he kicked the door closed with his boot and sat her on the bed. Without waiting for her to undress, he was on her.

Unlacing his breeches with one hand, he shoved up her skirts with the other. "No panties?" he asked, his hands skimming up her thighs.

She grabbed the hem of his shirt and pulled it over his head. "Figured they'd only get in the way."

"Mmmm. Clever girl." He parted her folds and expertly rubbed her clit with his finger and thumb.

She arched into him, needing to feel more of him there, and he didn't disappoint.

His fingers glided through her slickness. A masculine sound rumbled in his chest. She was so ready for him, and he knew it.

He kissed her hard, possessively. She was his and he was hers. And nothing would ever get between them again.

He gripped the base of his magnificent cock, and she felt it at her center, parting her folds. With several slow, shallow movements, he coated himself with her liquid heat. Then, without breaking their kiss, he thrust hard.

She cried out in sheer ecstasy as this amazingly courageous man filled her completely. She clung to him, not wanting to let go of him—ever.

Despite his earlier doubts, in the past few months, he'd become an incredible father and role model to their son who loved and adored him. As far as Darius was concerned, his dad hung the moon and the stars and could do no wrong. Even though today had made it official, Vince was already a trusted member of the Iron Guild, having mapped several more unknown portals.

She ran her hands over his broad back, over his many scars, feeling the movement of his powerful muscles contract beneath her fingertips.

The boy she'd fallen in love with all those years ago was everything she'd dreamed he would be as a man.

"Tell me you're close," he rasped in her ear.

"I am, my love."

His rhythm changed slightly. With each thrust, he pushed in deeper, holding it a little longer before sliding back. He was on the brink now, just as she was. It hadn't taken long. It never did.

And then...

A rush of intense pleasure crashed over her, radiating outward from where there were joined.

And then...

His muscles tensed, her name roaring from his lips as he came.

"Wow," she said when she was finally able to think and speak coherently. "That was...wow."

He nuzzled her neck, kissing that ticklish spot just below her ear and making her shiver. "I know."

They lay contentedly in each other's arms. She cracked open one eye and found that he was staring at her, his gaze roving over her face as if he'd never seen her before.

"What?" she asked, feeling almost self-conscious.

"You're so beautiful like this," he said, running the backs of his fingers along her cheek. "I used to dream of the day when I would see you again. Make love to you again. Draw you again."

Seemed like both a long time ago and just yesterday when he'd sketched her in that daisy-filled field. "I'll look for some art supplies in the market tomorrow."

"I would love that," he said, falling onto the pillow beside her.

He'd either be asleep in a few minutes or be ready for another round of lovemaking. She'd better tell him now.

She pushed a piece of hair off his sweaty forehead. "Vince?"

"Mmmm." His eyes were closed.

"That thing I wanted to talk to you about?"

"Yeah?"

She took a deep breath. "Well, the thing is...I'm pregnant."

His eyes popped open and he frowned. "What?"

"I'm going to have another baby."

His expression was completely unreadable. Was he angry? Upset?

"But...how...?" He sat up and scrubbed a hand over his face. "I mean, I know how, but..."

Her hands began to shake. He wasn't excited. "You're upset. I'm—"

In a flash, he dropped to his knees on floor beside the bed and took her hands in his as if he were praying to her.

"Upset? Zara, the Fates have given me the most perfect woman in two worlds to love and cherish. I'm consumed by you. Hell. I'd spend twenty-four seven in this bed with you if I could. How could I be upset that you're pregnant when I find you utterly impossible to resist? Holy Fates! I'm going to be a father again! A father!"

She felt as if her heart would burst.

Lifting her into his arms, he spun her around and they laughed. Tears stung the backs of her eyes. She'd read him wrong. He wasn't upset—he was ecstatic.

When he stopped, his eyes sparkled with emotion. "I love you, Zara. With all my heart and soul, I love you."

She wrapped her arms tighter around his neck and pressed her lips to his. "And you, my warrior, I love you, too."

Don't miss the next book in the Iron Portal series: Toryn and Keely's spicy romance in *HEARTLESS REBEL*. My most favorite meet-cute I've written is in this book!

Sign up for my VIP reader list to be the first to know about my new releases, sales, freebies and other fun goodies (like an Iron Portal coloring page).

http://laurielondonbooks.com/mailing-list-sign-up/

If you enjoyed **Hidden Warrior** and would like to help the series grow, please consider leaving a brief review at your favorite online bookseller and/or Goodreads. Reviews, even if it's just a line or two, help other readers discover my books and decide if they'd like them too. Thank you!

EXCERPT FROM HEARTLESS REBEL

Tormented by a savage past and shattered by a bitter betrayal, Iron Guild warrior Toryn Flynn trusts no one and cares about nothing except the battle against their enemies. His target: a mobster who finances deadly missions into Cascadia.

Kicked out of the house by her puritanical father, Keely Weber and her sister run a bookstore and fortune-telling business in an underground district in New Seattle—until a powerful man who controls the area kidnaps Keely's sister to sell her into the Talent sex-trade.

When a beautiful woman literally falls into his arms, Toryn realizes she holds the key to his success. Keely will do anything to rescue her sister...including taking risks with a dangerously sexy man who pushes all her buttons.

From the gritty streets of the city's underbelly to a sexual-fantasy-themed island, passions ignite. But with evil surrounding them and time running out, Toryn must decide whether to sacrifice the woman he's falling for or dare to trust his heart again.

———

Keely needed to sell this kiss.

She gave it everything she had, which wasn't too hard given that the stranger she was kissing was smoking hot.

With her mouth pressed to his, she ran her hands up the muscular plane of his chest, over his leather jacket, and wrapped her arms around his neck. He tasted and smelled amazing—like whiskey and mint, one hundred percent male. She'd always been impulsive, but she'd never done anything quite like this before.

At first his mouth had been rigid, but then his lips softened and began to move against hers, his hand slipped into her hair. The guy was actually kissing her back!

Good. It made this all the more believable.

All she had to do was make it seem like *she* wasn't the woman her pursuers were after. *That* woman had been alone and wearing a faded grey sweatshirt with the hood pulled up. *This* woman wore a blue tank top, had longish red hair that fell past her shoulders, and was engaging in some serious PDA with her boyfriend.

Two totally different people, right? God, she hoped so.

From the corner of her eye, she saw her two pursuers sprint around the corner. They were coming right this way.

For a moment she questioned her split-second decision to stop running and try outsmarting them. She was desperate. She just hoped she hadn't been *too* desperate.

Acutely aware of how high the stakes were, she kissed the stranger with even more intensity. She couldn't let those men from the club, those thugs, get ahold of her, otherwise where would that leave her sister? It wouldn't do either of them any good if they were *both* being held against their will. Plus, this was all her fault. She needed to make this kiss work.

Hitching a knee, she hooked her leg around the man's hip. It shocked the hell out of her when he cupped his hands under her butt and pulled her other leg up, wrapping them both around his waist.

"Thank you," she whispered against his lips.

"You're welcome," he said, his low, rough voice reverberating through her body like a tuning fork.

Her pursuers drew closer. She could feel them looking in this direction. Instinctively, she put up a mental shield, sending invisible jolts of electricity racing down her arms.

The stranger's body shifted slightly.

He hadn't felt that, had he? No, he was reaching for something.

Without breaking the kiss, he turned them so that her back was against the wall. His large frame now stood between her and those men.

Was he protecting her?

Something flashed close to her face.

He had a knife!

Panic and confusion shot through her.

"Shhh. This isn't for you." He ran a thumb over the pulse point on her neck.

His touch was intoxicating and she felt herself relax, although she didn't drop her guard. Almost immediately, he hauled her closer and deepened the kiss, stroking his hand through her hair. He pressed her mouth wider and slipped his tongue inside, acting as if she was his to take. Heat seared through her and desire pooled low in her belly.

Oh God. What was going on? This was all just for show, and yet it felt so...*real*.

Her heart pounded furiously as the two men jogged past them on the sidewalk, not more than a few feet away. She couldn't tell if her physical reaction was entirely because of them or this darkly compelling man she was kissing.

The moment her pursuers disappeared around the corner, the man took a step backwards and released her. The blade he'd held a moment ago was gone. She disentangled herself, feeling suddenly awkward.

Now that she was staring up at him from a distance

greater than the length of an eyelash, her breath caught in her throat.

He stood a good head taller than her, with sleek raven hair pulled into a low bun, warm olive skin and the most intense gray eyes she'd ever seen. He wore a black leather jacket, a plaid shirt underneath, low-slung jeans and black boots with thick soles. If someone were to ask her what two plus two was right now, she'd probably tell them her middle name.

"Um...thanks. I really appreciate...what you did." Sure, he'd just saved her ass, but that was, quite possibly, the most amazing kiss in the history of the world.

"What the hell was that?" he asked, anger flashing in his eyes.

And just like that, her balloon popped.

———

Find out what happens next in HEARTLESS REBEL, available now!

ALSO BY LAURIE LONDON

Iron Portal Series

DARK ASSASSIN

MIDNIGHT ROGUE

HIDDEN WARRIOR

HEARTLESS REBEL

Sweetblood Series

BONDED BY BLOOD

EMBRACED BY BLOOD

TEMPTED BY BLOOD

SEDUCED BY BLOOD

HIDDEN BY BLOOD

ENCHANTED BY BLOOD

ENTICED BY BLOOD

UNRAVELED BY BLOOD

Nocturne Falls Universe

HOW KNOT TO MARRY A VAMPIRE

ABOUT THE AUTHOR

Laurie London is the bestselling author of the Sweetblood and Iron Portal series—dark, sexy paranormal romance, set primarily in the Pacific Northwest. Publisher's Weekly has called her work "sexy" and "sizzling."

Laurie lives on a small town outside of Seattle with her family. Armed with a business degree, she worked for a Fortune 500 company in IT and as an underwriter. After a hiatus to raise two children and a variety of animals, she studied, apprenticed for and became a licensed optician. Her other jobs included cocktail waitress, hotel maid, candy store manager and bridal gown sales, so she is well qualified to be a writer.

Find Laurie online:
www.LaurieLondonBooks.com